DON'T GO KNOTTING MY HEART

MONSTERVILLE, USA

AVA ROSS

DON'T GO KNOTTING MY HEART

Monsterville, USA, 4

Cover art by Wolfraven Studio

Editing/Proofreading by JA Wren & Owl Eyes Proofs & Edits

FOREWORD

A note to the reader.

If you found this book outside of Amazon,
it's likely a stolen/pirated copy.
Authors make nothing when books are pirated.
If authors are not paid for their work,
they can't afford to keep writing.

*For my parents who
always believed I could do this.*

SERIES BY AVA

Mail-Order Brides of Crakair

Brides of Driegon

Fated Mates of the Ferlaern Warriors

Fated Mates of the Xilan Warriors

Holiday with a Cu'zod Warrior

Galaxy Games

Alien Warrior Abandoned

Beastly Alien Boss

Bride of the Fae

A Sci-fi Holiday Tail

Monsterville, USA

Monster on Board
(Co-written with Alana Khan)

A Monster Worth Fighting For
(Monster Between the Sheets)

Third Galaxy on the Left

You can find my books on Amazon.

DON'T GO KNOTTING MY HEART

**I'm falling for a wolf shifter,
but my past may endanger us both.**

I escaped a life of fear for the beautiful mountainous town of Monsterville, where I meet Storm, a gorgeous wolf shifter. His wolfish ways and heady kisses draw me in, and the future he offers, one full of peace and love, makes me long for a life I never thought I'd find.

He invites me to a wolf pack reunion, where things between us only get better. But my past haunts me, and if I don't flee, they'll drag me back and lock me up in a place where Storm will never find me.

Don't Go Knotting My Heart is set in the Monsterville, USA world. Each book is standalone and can be read in any order. Expect romantic hijinks with monsters, heat, and a happily ever after.

Check out the rest of the Monsterville, USA world!

Candy for My Orc Boss
Orc Me Baby One More Time
Gargoyles Just Want to Have Fun
Don't Go Knotting My Heart
Whose Bed Have Your Claws Been Under?
Uptown Ogre
Oops, I Elf'd it Again
My Orc-y Breaky Heart
Hold Me Closer, Fiery Phoenix
Who Let the Demon Out?
Monsterville

CHAPTER 1
LUNA

When I moved to Monsterville to escape the jaws of my brother's trap, I never expected to enjoy my new town as much as I did. It was ironic that I loved it here. Monsters gave me a feeling of peace and happiness I hadn't found with the humans I'd left behind.

I had a new home. A new way of life.

A new name.

Would I be able to stay here longer than the last few places I'd fled to? Only time would tell.

I'd hate to have to run again now that I'd finally found a town I loved.

I jogged along the path winding through the forest on the edge of town, my feet pounding rhythmically on the dirt. The woods around me were alive with the sounds of birds chirping and squirrels scolding me for disturbing their peace. Fallen leaves crunched beneath my sneakers, releasing a pungent, earthy smell that brought back memories of childhood days spent jumping into leaf piles and snuggling in front of the fireplace afterward, sipping hot cocoa.

Being close to nature brought peace to my turbulent world. There was no better way to clear my head and replenish my soul.

I breathed in the crisp, clean air and my spirits lifted.

When I rounded a bend in the path, I spied a big silver wolf standing about forty feet away, his paws braced on the soil and his glorious ruff whispering in the breeze.

My pace slowed until I came to a stop. I stared at him while he watched me.

It couldn't be a real wolf. Yes, Monsterville is nestled in a valley surrounded by wild mountains so tall that snow capped them almost all year round. I'd heard bears lived high in the hills, but I'd read real wolves no longer lived in this area.

Only wolf *shifters*.

As a dog lover, I could appreciate how majestic this creature was, from his thick silver fur to his bushy tail. He was huge; the top of his head must come to my mid-chest.

No "real" wolf had mossy green eyes.

I could tell he was male by his large size and his broad chest and head. Just like I'd seen in domesticated dogs, females were often narrower in build. He also had prominent facial features, including a blocky muzzle.

For a moment, our gazes locked, and I sensed a variety of emotions in his beautiful eyes. Excitement.

Longing. And a hint of sorrow that struck through my heart like a blade.

I started toward him, *compelled* to go to him, but before I reached him, he turned and trotted into the dense vegetation along the trail.

After I waited, barely breathing, to see if he'd reappear, I continued running, and while I listened, I didn't hear him following.

I did sense him watching, as if he'd climbed up onto a ledge above and peered down at me, keeping me safe from the dangers of the forest. I ran faster, feeling safer and stronger, more alive than I had in years.

Rounding a bend, I slowed my pace to a walk to creep across a section where the ground had washed away during a prior storm. Stones scattered from beneath my feet, plinking over the edge on my right, falling down the steep, rocky cliff.

I'd nearly crossed the rough stretch when the ground shifted. It gave way beneath my feet, and my breath caught. My ankle twisted, and my sharp cry rang out as agony shot up my leg.

Birds screeched and darted into the air as I scrambled to regain my footing despite the stabbing pain in my leg. Plummeting downward, I tried to grab stubby trees, but only stripped off the dead leaves. I tumbled, smacking into fallen trees and big rocks. I landed with a hard thud at the bottom of a ravine; the wind knocked out of me.

I lay on my belly for a moment with my limbs splayed out, dazed and confused. A quick internal assessment showed my right temple hurt, and the trickle down my cheek told me I was bleeding, though not profusely. My ankle throbbed, but other than a few stinging places on my arms and sides, it appeared I hadn't damaged myself too badly.

Lifting my upper body, I winced at the cut in my right palm. I peered up the cliff and sighed to see how far I'd have to climb to reach the path.

No time like the present.

I carefully rolled over onto my butt and clutched my head until it stopped spinning. Maybe the blow I'd taken had done more damage than I thought.

A glance around showed me I'd landed at the base of a tiny valley with steep sides creating a pocket in the forest. A trickle of a stream ran down one cliff face. The water traveled across the low area about twenty feet before disappearing into the ground near a big boulder. At least I hadn't hit the boulder before I came to a stop.

I grabbed onto the scruffy tree beside me and used it to pull myself to my feet. My ankle gave way, and I groaned as I fell to the ground again, hitting my hip hard on a rock.

My eyes stinging with tears, I rolled onto my back and stared at the sky. I'd left my car in the lot at the base of the trail, but I'd run about two miles, planning to turn around soon and return to the lot long before the sun set.

Was I stuck here?

Absolutely not. No matter what situation I found myself in, I'd never give up. Giving up meant stepping into my worst nightmares.

"Crawl," I whispered. Rising to my hands and knees, I

started up the side that wasn't as steep as the others, trying over and over, but I kept hitting soft spots where the topsoil had washed away and slipping backward.

Finally, I stopped trying. Quitting was never an option, but it was clear I wasn't going to be able to climb out of this trap.

If I'd learned nothing else in my twenty-seven years, it was that I could only have the life I wanted if I grabbed onto it with both hands. But with each attempt, I lost more of my strength. My body trembled, and my ankle throbbed. There was no harm in resting for a moment, regrouping.

Someone would pass on the path. I'd hear them, call out, and they'd rescue me.

I unclipped my fanny pack because the bump hurt where it pressed into my spine, and laid it beside me, grateful I'd brought a few basic things that could make a difference in my survival. If only I'd remembered to charge my phone last night. By the time I reached the lot at the base of the mountains, I realized the battery was pretty much dead. Rather than carry it, I left it in my car. A bad move on my part.

"Help," I cried, rising to my hands and knees again. I screamed, over and over, hoping someone was near enough to hear.

Only the chatter of chipmunks and the low call of a dove broke the silence in between each of my yells.

Again, I tried to climb out of the ravine, but like before, I kept sliding back to where I started.

Since it appeared I was stuck here for a while, I

leaned against the cliff face and cradled my face in my palms. The sun hitched toward the horizon and a sliver of a moon rose, peering down at me. Clouds skirted across the sky, and a bitter wind dipped through the ravine, determined to drain me of heat. My teeth chattered, and shivers wracked my frame.

Unzipping my pouch, I pulled out the tiny pen flashlight I'd tucked inside ages ago. Darkness brought danger, as I'd learned when I was young. Out here, the odds of the predator who'd tried to hurt me when I was ten finding me were slim but being able to pierce the night with a light as tiny as this made my heartrate slow and my breathing less ragged.

I kept crying out, hoping someone would hear, but no one answered.

Because I wasn't completely useless, I dragged fallen branches covered with dead leaves closer and cleared the ground beneath where I might be forced to lay all night.

Quivers tracked through me. I wore a snug tank and leggings, and they would not be enough to keep me warm tonight. Pulling my thin windbreaker from the pouch, I put it on, feeling only marginally warmer.

As the sun slipped away, stealing my calm, I struggled not to cry.

I laid down and tugged the leaf-covered branches over me. At least they blocked some of the wind.

Brush rustled near the boulder, and I lifted my head, peering in that direction. Golden eyes gleamed in the moonlight. They started moving toward me.

My heart leapt into my throat. I scrambled up the

cliff face, crying out in terror when I slipped back to the ground.

A glance over my shoulder showed the creature still creeping closer, the thuds of its feet shifting leaves and sticks.

"No," I cried. "Go away." I grabbed a rock and threw it, but it skidded across the ground a foot or so away from the glowing eyes. Whatever it was didn't flinch. It kept coming, creeping closer. A low growl rang out, echoing around me.

With a stick in my hand, I crawled along the base of the cliff, moving away from the creature, hoping to find a place to hide.

My head bumped into something. I shrieked.

Tumbling backward, I fell on my back. Whimpers ripped up my throat as whatever I'd run into stepped toward me, over me. Clouds parted, and moonlight stabbed down, revealing the wolf I'd seen on the trail earlier.

It leapt off me and raced toward the creature. The beast who'd stalked me cried out and ran in the opposite direction, scrambling behind the boulder with the wolf following. Barks and snarls rang out as the two battled.

Silence descended. I huddled against the cliff, my teeth chattering. The adrenaline I'd relied on when I tried to climb out of this trap had long since bled away. I was a wreck, and all I wanted to do was sob.

Leaves crackled and a stick snapped from the other side of the ravine.

The wolf appeared in the moonlight. He trotted over

to where I'd originally laid beneath the branches and sniffed the ground. He picked up my pack in his teeth and brought it to me, dropping it at my feet. After dragging the branches over and laying them beside me, he nudged his snout forward, briefly touching my nose in a wolfish kiss.

Despite his recent defense, raw fear spiked up my spine. I should try to run, but I sensed he meant me no harm. He'd protected me from the other creature, and now he was setting me up for the night.

"If you're a shifter, could you turn back into your human form?" I asked, my voice quaking. "I'm scared."

He nudged my pack closer and lifted a branch, dragging the thickest part over me.

When I was completely covered, he lifted the branches with his snout enough to crawl beneath them. He settled down beside me with a heavy sigh, resting his snout on my thigh.

I tentatively touched the top of his head, and he huffed and leaned into my hand.

"Are you like a domesticated dog?" I whispered. "They enjoy having their ears rubbed."

I boldly did so, and he grunted and lifted a paw onto my thighs, slow-creeping up over me until his warmth covered me like a thick, silver-furred blanket.

"You're heavy," I said with a soft laugh, still scratching his ears. "But I'm so glad you're here with me. You saved me from that horrible beast."

He woofed as if he laughed.

"Well, maybe not a big beast. Whatever it was," I said. "It was coming closer. It might've bitten me."

He seemed to nod.

Opening my pack, I pulled out the protein bar I'd tucked inside earlier, saving my small bag of nuts for later. I ripped into the package and broke off half, offering it to the wolf, but he turned his nose away.

"Aren't you hungry?" I asked.

He snorted.

Maybe not. Hungry, I ate it all, and I was tempted to lick out the inside of the package. I washed it down with a few swallows from the small water bottle clipped to my pack, grateful I'd listened when others said to never run without taking basic supplies.

I'd never go running without a fully charge phone again, however.

Sated for now, I scooted lower, laying down and tucking the leafy branches around us. He eased onto the ground beside me, pressing his full length against the front of my body so I could spoon him. I marveled at how big he was, his body longer than mine when he stretched out.

With my pack as a pillow, I dozed.

The temperature dropped, but only brief shivers took over my frame, and those were mostly generated by fear. My wolf kept me safe and warm, and with that thought, I drifted into a deep sleep.

I woke with a start and sat up, knocking the branches off as I peered around. Dawn sunlight bled yellow and orange across the horizon.

The wolf was gone.

After taking a sip of water and eating a few nuts, I tackled the cliff again, but I still couldn't reach the path. My sore ankle throbbed; it wouldn't hold all my weight.

I'd settled back in my nest when a shout rang out on the path above.

"Help," I cried. I struggled to rise to my feet, groaning as pain shot up my leg. "Help me. I'm down here!"

"Here," someone yelled, their footsteps coming closer. "I heard her."

A man and a woman in rescue gear peered over the top of the ravine, their faces creased with concern.

"Are you Luna Hallsworth?" the woman shout.

Three months ago? No.

Today?

"Yes," I said, tears of relief streaming down my face. "That's me. Luna. I fell. I hurt my ankle. Please. Can you help me?"

"Coming down," the guy said, and the reassurance in his voice made my chest ache. Sobs rose in my throat, and I sat on the ground, clutching my arms to my chest.

I was safe.

For now.

CHAPTER 2
STORM

"Would you be willing to do something for me?" I asked my gargoyle best friend, Goreg.

"What would that be?" he asked as he connected wires to a panel in the big barn behind the B&B where he and his wife now lived together. From what I could tell, their marriage had been hasty. He'd had a crush on her for a while, but as far as I knew, he hadn't said even two words to her in the six weeks or so since he first saw her around town. Suddenly, though, they were married.

But he and Violet couldn't keep their hands off each other—or claws, in Goreg's case—so I'd say it all worked out as it should.

"Would you pretend to be my owner?" I scratched the back of my neck and braced myself for his sharp no.

"Owner?" Turning, he leaned against the wall, pinching his big, folded wings between his body and the unfinished sheetrock behind him.

"See, there's this woman," I said.

His dusky blue face creased with a grin. "Luna."

"How do you know her name?"

"She passes by the house every day with one dog or another."

"She's a dog walker."

"And you're a dog."

"Wolf shifter," I barked, then scowled at his ongoing grin.

"Last I knew," he said, "you saw her weeks ago and took off like the wolfhounds of hell were after you."

"The wolfhounds of hell never come after wolf shifters. We're too close to their species."

"See?" He scratched his knobby head. "I didn't even realize wolfhounds of hell existed."

"Why wouldn't they?" I asked. "Back to you owning me. As I said, Luna has a dog walking business. She also boards dogs and has a grooming business."

Goreg chuckled. "And you'd like her to groom you."

"Sounds creepy, doesn't it?" I winced, and my shoulders slumped. "Never mind."

"Why don't you walk up to her and introduce yourself?" He turned and started working on the panel again.

"We've already met."

"Then why are you here bugging me and not letting her groom you?"

I rolled my eyes. "She doesn't know I'm the wolf who rescued her in the woods."

"I believe there's a story there you haven't shared with me yet."

Since he was my best friend, I told him almost everything. For some reason, I'd held this back.

I explained about seeing Luna in the woods, a totally innocent thing. I'd been out for a run myself when I heard someone running behind me on the trail.

And, yeah, I followed her once I saw her, but only to make sure she was alright. It was getting dark. The parking lot was empty except for our two cars. And the woods were a dangerous place, a proven fact when the ground gave way and she fell into that ravine.

"Why didn't you shift into yourself and reassure her?" Goreg asked, connecting wires to the panel. "Introduce yourself?"

"I couldn't."

He shot a lifted brow glance over his shoulder. "Why not?"

"Because then she would've known it was me."

"Isn't that the point we're driving toward right now?"

"No." I frowned. "I guess I was nervous."

"About what?"

"You know my past, how I was crazy about someone who died."

"You said you were a teenager."

"It could've turned into more than just friends." I still missed Marlie. I would for the rest of my days. Our packs shared the same territory, and her parents were good friends with mine. We'd been born about the same time and played together from the time we could crawl.

"Is she the only one you'll ever love?" Goreg asked,

shooting a look toward me again, his claws resting on the panel.

"No." I knew that in my heart. We might've ended up mates or only great friends. "She died before we had a chance to find out."

"I'd say you're mixed up about how you should feel about Luna, then. Great name, by the way. It totally fits."

"Yeah. The moon and all. She's not a shifter, though. She smells pure human."

"And your pack is okay with you potentially dating someone who's not a shifter?"

"Sure. No one cares about something like that." The packs weren't like his gargoyle parents who'd frowned on him marrying outside his species.

"If you want my advice," Goreg said, "walk up to her in this form. Say hi. Introduce yourself. You don't need me to help you with that. It's easy."

"Says the gargoyle who took off before the female he liked could introduce herself," I said with a shake of my head.

Goreg grumbled. "That was then."

"Rather than 'walk up to her and say hi,' as you suggest, you lurked on pretty much every building in town hoping just to see Violet."

"That was still then. I *did* talk to her eventually."

I sighed. "It's easy to say do it when your heart isn't involved."

"You're that into her already?"

"She's wonderful."

"Like, take her home to the pack wonderful or friendship wonderful?"

"Totally take her back to the pack wonderful."

"Alright then," he said, placing his tools in the leather bag sitting on the wooden floorboards. "I'll take you into town and hook you up with the groomer."

We went inside the B&B so he could tell Violet where we were going. Stopping in the big foyer that was open all the way to the roof, he called out her name.

"Hey," she said, leaning over the second-floor railing. Before he could speak, she climbed onto the rail and swan dove into the air.

They'd done this before, so I didn't brace myself for her to go splat. I leaned against the wall and watched as Goreg's wings extended and he leapt into flight, swooping up to snatch her out of the air. By the time he landed on the foyer carpet, their mouths were fused together, and her legs were wrapped around his waist.

I wanted to growl, but envy filled me instead.

I did think about Marlie a lot, but since I saw Luna for the first time, my focus had centered on her. A wolf knew things like this. She could be the one I'd love until my dying day.

I had to get to know her better to find out.

The packs had a big reunion planned soon. Should I invite her? I guess I'd have to talk to her first.

Finally, Violet and Goreg parted, and he lowered her to the floor, telling her he and I were going into town for a bit.

"When will you be back?" she asked, nodding in greeting to me.

"Before you miss me," Goreg said.

"Too late," she said in a bubbly voice. "I miss you already."

I rolled my eyes. Really. I loved that my friend was happy, but could we get this going before I turned gray?

They kissed some more. I stared at the carpet. Eventually, we went out to their car and got inside.

"When do you plan to shift?" he asked, glancing my way as he drove toward Luna's business. "And you know most people need an appointment for a grooming."

"Maybe she takes walk-ins."

"That's usually for humans and hair stylists."

"Thank you for doing this," I said. "I know it sounds weird."

"You saved my butt with Violet when my brothers moved in with us."

His gargoyle brothers had been carved from pure mischief. He and Violet had just gotten married, and Violet triggered a gargoyle custom that invited them to stay as long as they'd like. I'd already told him I'd stop by, but I offered to remain while his brothers were there and get their kitchen in order. I ran my own restaurant, so it was easy to make suggestions about appliances and cabinets, food to stock. The B&B had been a wreck when they moved in.

"I'd do it again," I said as he pulled into the business's parking lot.

We sat in the vehicle, him leaving the engine running and the heater on since it was cold outside.

He glanced my way. "Now would be the time to shift unless you want me to put a collar on you in human form, walk you inside, and hand the leash to her."

That idea had merit, but I wasn't ready to meet her as myself yet.

I closed my eyes and let my wolf form override the human.

"I still think that's cool," Goreg said. "I know. I'm a freakin' gargoyle, complete with leathery skin, claws, and wings, but to have your sleek, furry form . . . To run through the woods and fuse with nature. I don't imagine there's anything like it." He grinned. "Here I go, running on and on when you want to go lick Luna's hand." Peering around, he frowned. "All I have is a piece of rope in the trunk. Will that do for a leash?"

I nodded.

With the rope around my neck, I padded placidly beside him into the building.

Luna looked up from where she was bathing a yorkie. She'd pulled her long blonde hair into a high ponytail, and as I took in her pretty blue eyes and delicate shape, I gave her a wolfy grin. Fates, I hoped I wasn't drooling. That wouldn't go over well.

The yorkie started barking and springing about in the tub, quivering with terror. Jeez. I wasn't going to eat her.

"Can I help you?" Luna asked in the sweetest, most dog-friendly voice I'd ever heard.

"Yes. I'm Goreg, and this is . . ." My friend's brow knit together. "Fluffy."

Ugh. We should've agreed on a name before I shifted.

"He's my dog," Goreg added. "Wolf. No, *dog*."

A smile teased across Luna's lips as she finished rinsing the yorkie and lifted her onto a table for drying. "You're sure?"

"Definitely a dog," Goreg said.

I sighed. Wolves were sleek. Strong. Majestic.

Dogs . . . drooled.

"He's Fluffy, the . . . big dog," Goreg said.

"Hi, Fluffy," Luna said in a high-pitched voice. "Aren't you a beauty?" Her laughing eyes met Goreg's. "I think I've seen him before. I just can't remember where."

She finished drying the yorkie and took her into an adjoining room where she must board the animals.

"Fluffy needs a grooming," Goreg said. At least he got that part right. "Do you have an opening today?"

"I do." Striding around the counter, she approached us. "Would you like a nice bath, big boy?"

"Oh, I'm sure he would," Goreg said with a laugh. He caught my eye, and I realized right then that the mischief gene had been passed not only to his brothers, but to my friend as well. "Do you express their butt glands as part of the grooming?"

Butt . . .? I was going to kill him.

"Of course." She took the rope from Goreg. "Why don't you come back in about an hour? We should be finished by then."

"Thanks." Goreg said. He gave me a quick tap on the head and left.

Luna and I were alone!

I tried not to bounce around like a puppy. I was finally close to her again. She was going to bathe me. We would—

She stooped down and wove her fingers into my ruff, holding my face still so our eyes could meet. "First, I owe you thanks, *Fluffy*. You saved my life that night, and I never got the chance to tell you how much it meant to me knowing you were there, protecting me."

Wait. She could tell that was me?

Straightening, she shot me a sharp look. "Now shift into your human form, or I'm shoving you out the door. You can hail your gargoyle friend for a ride home."

CHAPTER 3
LUNA

If he thought he could pull a fast one on me—

He shifted, and I learned the answer to the question I'd researched extensively online but couldn't find.

When a wolf shifter changed back into his human form, his clothing came with him.

He was cute, so I was kind of disappointed he didn't reappear naked.

"Tell me what's going on," I said, my fist on my hip. Stella, the yorkie, yipped in her crate. "It's okay, sweetie," I called out. "The big bad wolf isn't going to bite you."

He sputtered.

"Cat got your tongue?" I asked, enjoying seeing him disconcerted. I'd seen this guy around town, though we hadn't formally met. Who could miss him? Stunning was one way to describe him. Gorgeous and sexy was another, from his thick chestnut hair pulled back at his nape to his tan skin and his mossy green eyes.

Those eyes had haunted me since the night he saved me.

"Sorry," he said, his palms splaying wide. "I shouldn't have done this."

My teasing smile fell. "Is this a joke between you and your friend?"

"Not at all."

"Explain, then. I assume you really *don't* want me to express your anal glands."

"I'm open to a bath and some grooming, but I'm hoping to avoid anal gland action."

I laughed, but quickly sobered. "That's not an explanation."

He sighed, and his gaze slid away from mine. "I wanted to meet you."

"In wolf form?"

"In any form."

"Then why the ruse?" My heart should not be softening, but he hadn't caused any harm.

"It was a mistake," he said. "I see that now. I should've come in without my friend and talked to you, asked you to do something with me for fun."

"Like what?"

His head tilted. "Want to go apple picking and make a pie?"

Now that would be an unusual date. "Most guys want a movie, dinner, and whatever else I'm willing to offer."

"I'm not most guys, though I'm open to offers."

I bet he was.

"I also wanted to make sure you were okay after your fall last week. The cliffs were steep. You hurt your ankle." He looked down at it. "How is it?"

"A sprain. It's getting better. It swells a little at night but propping it up on a pillow and icing it helps."

"You should have it on a pillow now."

I waved to the sinks where I bathed dogs and the adjoining room where I housed animals in crates. Out back, I'd set up runs for the dogs and catios for kitties who enjoyed going outside while being boarded. "I can't keep my leg up all the time. I have to work."

"As for that night," he huffed out, "I wanted to carry you out of that ravine, but there was no way I would've been able to make it up the cliff."

"Then why didn't you go get help? You could've left me." My mind would've screamed with panic, but it made the most sense.

"Because a bobcat lives inside the small cave behind the boulder."

The warmth left my face. "The creature stalking toward me was a bobcat?" They rarely attacked humans, but I'd fallen into its territory. There was no telling what it might've done if he hadn't been there.

"It was a hissy thing like most cats, but I didn't dare leave you alone with it."

"You left me alone in the morning." I couldn't stop my voice from lightening. Was I ready to forgive him for not revealing himself that night? He could be a shy wolf shifter. He'd kind of proven that already by asking his friend to bring him in while in wolf form.

"I chased the bobcat for miles until I was sure it wouldn't return before I could go get help."

"You didn't have a phone on you."

"Neither did you."

"It needed a charge." I huffed. "Tell you what. Let's take some dogs for walks. We can talk."

"Alright."

I leashed Stella and a fluffy Maltese named Fred, and we took them outside.

"Woodland trail or the sidewalk?" I asked, nudging my head to the woods behind the small building where I leased space for my business.

He stared into the woods for a long time before turning to the road passing the building. "The sidewalk will be smoother for your ankle, won't it? Let's not strain it."

"Thank you."

We walked, me with Fred, him with Stella dancing around his ankles. She'd gotten over her fear of the big bad wolf and was now contemplating running his fan club. I couldn't blame her. If she asked, I'd probably join myself.

"You didn't tell me your name," I said.

"Storm."

"Unusual, but I like it."

He nodded. "Luna's amazing."

I grinned. "Because you're a wolf shifter. I imagine the moon plays a big part in your life."

"Contrary to mythology, we can shift whenever we please. We're different from werewolves that are forcibly changed based on the moon's cycle."

"Werewolves are real?" I asked, incredulous.

"Sure, though I haven't heard there were any around for ages. Could be they've died out. We invite them to join our packs, but they're often feral and need watching."

That sounded scary. But . . .

"It must be amazing to be a wolf shifter," I said, envy lifting my voice. "If you bite someone, do they turn into wolves too?"

He crooked his neck so he could watch me as we walked. "You almost sound like you'd be interested in something like that."

The sun shone down, making the fall day almost feel warm, though I was grateful I wore a thick coat. Soon, I'd need gloves and a hat. I couldn't wait for snow to blanket the world in white.

I lifted my chin. "Maybe I am." It would allow me to completely escape. My family would never find me if I could race through the woods in an animal form. I'd keep running and hiding until they completely lost my scent.

"Then I'm sad to tell you no." He glanced at me. "Sorry?"

"No biting, then," I said with a slump of my shoulders.

Humor sparked in his eyes. "Oh, I never said that." His voice dropped to a deep husky tone that made sparks shoot through me. "I'd be happy to demonstrate any day of the week."

"We barely know each other," I said, though, wow. I almost wanted to dare him to do it.

He slapped his palm on his chest. "How can you say that after we slept together?'

I nudged his shoulder with mine. "Funny." Because it was entertaining to tease him, I kept going. "It would've been more interesting if you hadn't been in wolf form."

He stopped on the sidewalk, staring forward. Stella leapt up onto his leg, whimpering. I almost wanted to do the same thing myself.

Why was I attracted to him so quickly? It must be that savior complex thing. I was grateful to him, so I was . . . I shook my head. No way would I fall for someone just because they kept me safe for a night. If I was falling, it was because I liked Storm.

He shot me a grin. "Do you mean that?"

Jittery about my unexplained emotions, I started walking again. "You'll have to keep at it if you want to find out."

"Fair enough." He watched a dark car pass us on the street. "I talked Goreg into bringing me to your shop because I wanted to get to know you better."

"I thought you wanted your coat brushed."

"Name the place and time, and I'll roll over so you can scratch my belly."

I shook my head at his teasing.

We walked through town, stopping at a friend's cupcake shop for a treat. The dogs hopped around, yipping in excitement until Rylee, the owner of *Love at*

First Bite, gave them each a tiny dog biscuit. A dog lover like me, she made them here herself.

"Cupcake?" she asked us with a smile, her gaze sliding from me to Storm. She winked at me, showing approval. We'd met a few weeks ago when I was out for a jog and was drawn to the sweet scent of cupcakes, and I'd become a regular at her shop.

If I could stay here, I'd pursue our friendship, something that probably was not going to happen.

"What flavor cupcake would you like?" I asked Storm. "We can share one if you want. They're huge."

"She knows I have a wonderful appetite," her orc husband, Gunner, said, coming out of the back with their little boy, Josh, toddling beside him. "If they were puny things, I'd finish them off with one bite." He hefted Josh and dropped him onto his big shoulder, and the little boy squealed and clung to one of his dad's horns.

"I love chocolate," Storm said. "But they all look amazing."

Josh strained forward; his arms outstretched toward Storm.

"Looks like you've got another fan," I said, chuckling. Dogs loving him hadn't surprised me. It was sweet to see little kids approved of him as well.

"Can I hold him?" Storm asked with longing.

"Sure," Gunner said, placing Josh on his feet. The young boy toddled around the counter and launched himself at Storm's legs. Storm lifted the boy and propped him on his hip.

"What kind of cupcake should we get?" Storm asked Josh.

"Dat one," Josh said, pointing.

"Chocolate with peanut butter frosting, it is." Storm grinned my way. "Unless you'd prefer another flavor, Luna. I'm sure this little guy has a second choice."

"And a third and a fourth," Rylee said. She nodded to me and rolled her eyes at Storm.

Cute guy alert. Got it. It was hard to resist a guy who loved dogs and children. Except . . . I struggled to cling to my smile while Rylee bagged our cupcake.

I loved it in Monsterville, but I worried I'd soon have to run.

How long before they found me?

Josh wiggled, and Storm put him down. The boy skipped around the counter and launched himself at Gunner again, who lifted him into his arms.

Storm paid for our cupcake.

"I was about to take this little guy home," Gunner told Rylee. "I'll start dinner when I get there."

"Thanks," she said, hugging him. They kissed, and the sweet and loving gesture made envy ripple through me.

Storm held up the bag with the cupcake. "First one outside gets to choose the top or the bottom." He tugged on the leash. "Come on, Stella, babe, it's time for a race."

"Wait," I called out, scooting after him with Fred yipping by my ankles. "You can't have the top."

Outside, he waited for me, sitting at a cute table with scrolling iron chairs. A chilly breeze skipped through town, but the sun hit the small nook, warming it up nicely.

"You can take the top or the bottom, Luna," he said with a sly smile. "Just name the place and the time and I'm with you."

"You." I dropped into the opposite seat. "You don't get all that amazing peanut butter frosting for yourself."

He gently tore the cake in half, making sure each of us had a top and a bottom, then handed one side to me.

Stella and Fred sat nearby, their tails flicking, gazing up at him with complete adoration.

"Frankly," he said, "I'd happily give you the entire cupcake if it brought out your smile."

I had to agree because I felt the same. I was having a lot of fun with Storm. Would I be given the chance to create something special with him?

We finished the cupcake and disposed of the trash, then continued our walk, chatting about inane things, enjoying each other's company. It felt natural being with him, and I wanted to get to know him better.

We turned a corner.

A black car with tinted windows idled by the curb on the opposite side of the street. Normally, I'd think nothing of it.

I'd only stayed ahead of my family by being hyper-alert.

My footsteps slowed, but when the car remained there and no one got out, my pulse returned to a normal rhythm.

CHAPTER 4
STORM

We walked the dogs for another half an hour or so, and as much as I wanted to make our time together last longer, I didn't want to push things. I liked Luna a lot, and I wanted to get to know her better. Coming on too strong might push her away.

But that didn't stop me from stopping by to visit two days later. I watched as she finished clipping a long-haired cat, leaning against the counter and cooing to the fluffball.

"They call this a lion cut," she said over her shoulder. "Maine Coon Cats tend to get mats in their long fur, so some owners bring them in for hairdos like this." She turned off the clippers and gave the kitty a solid brushing.

The cat blinked at me, and like any other time I encountered a Coon, I sensed it watched me, waiting to see if I could be trusted. These cats could grow big, and this one had to be thirty pounds.

Turning with the cat in her arms, Luna lowered the beast onto a stainless-steel table to put him on display.

"See?" she said, stroking his spine. "Lion cut."

The fur on the main part of his body had been clipped short. His fluffy legs remained, as did the "mane" around its neck, plus a poof at the end of his tail.

"Aren't you comfier now, Teddy?" she asked, crooning at the cat who bobbed his orange and white striped head against her chin. "Coons can be incredibly sweet. This one's a love bug." She kissed the top of Teddy's head and nuzzled his neck.

I envied the cat.

The door opened behind me, a bell above it jingling.

"Teddy, baby!" a pretty woman with pretty auburn hair scooted around the counter and lifted Teddy up, turning him this way and that. "You look amazing." She held the cat to her chest, smiling at Luna. "Wonderful. Thank you so much for fitting him in. Silly boy won't let me groom him. He tolerates it for a few seconds before mischief fills his eyes and he tries to rip my hand apart." She shot me a smile. "I'm Paige, by the way. I recently moved to Monsterville and took a position at a local law firm."

"This is Storm," Luna said. "He stopped by . . ."

"To take you apple picking and then make a pie," I jumped into say. "Once you're finished for the day, that is." And assuming she was willing to take me up on the offer I'd made the other day.

Luna looked from me to Paige, who was waving my way and nodding. I grinned. Thanks for the help.

"I'm done," Luna said. "Teddy was my last grooming of the day." She rang Paige's bill up, and her friend paid.

"We're still on for boarding in December, correct?" Paige asked. "I'm the maid of honor in the holiday wedding of an old friend who lives in Screaming Woods."

A town where monsters were transformed in a lab, not born. I'd only heard a little about it, though the town wasn't far from here. A scientist went rogue and experimented on a few people in town. To the confusion of those living in Petrified Woods, those experimented on turned into monsters. But that happened a while ago.

"I lived in Petrified Woods until I was sixteen and my parents . . ." Shadows filled her green eyes. "They were scared about what happened, and they took me away. I haven't been back since. I just . . ." Her eyes closed and her face filled with sorrow. Even Teddy sensed the change in her feelings and placed a big paw on her face. Her eyes opened again, and they shimmered with tears. "My best friend was one of those experimented on, and he died. I couldn't bear to visit if he wasn't going to be there. It would hurt too much, you know? Being in the places we went together."

"And now you're returning for a wedding," I said softly, my heart aching for her.

"Yup." She nodded, her spine tightening. "She and I reconnected on Facebook. When she asked, I couldn't bear not to be a part of her wedding. So here I am, returning to the town I ran from."

"I hope it goes well for you," I said. "And I hope while

you're there, you can remember the fun things you did with him to balance the sad."

"That's what I'm hoping for too," she said, pressing her face into Teddy's fur.

"You know Teddy's always welcome here," Luna said gently, scratching Teddy's neck. The cat's purr echoed in the room. "I've got him down on my calendar. Don't worry about him at all."

"Thanks," Paige said. "I'm sure I'll run into you before then." She handed Teddy to me and hugged Luna. "I appreciate you so much," she whispered.

Teddy blinked up at me, his gaze sharp but more as if he was still analyzing me. I understood why. Wolves and cats were not often friends. But when I rubbed the side of his neck, his eyelids slid shut, and he purred.

"You've got the magic touch," Paige said, taking Teddy back. She placed him in a big carrier usually used for a medium-sized dog and started for the door. As she passed me, she grinned and paused, leaning close to say softly. "All the best, there, Storm. Luna's wonderful."

She was.

Paige left, and I leaned against the counter again.

"Let me make sure my boarding friends are happy, and then we can leave. After I settle them, I won't need to return until tomorrow morning. I have cameras on each animal, and I'll watch them from an app on my phone."

I helped her ensure their runs were clean, and that they had plenty of food and water.

She locked the front door and glanced around. "Isn't it getting too dark to pick apples?"

The sun hovered on the horizon, shooting pink and gold beams into the sky. Darkness would take over within half an hour.

"They strung twinkle lights all around the orchard," I said. "It's festive. But if you'd rather call it a day and go home, I understand."

She grinned up at me. "But you're a prized chef, and you said you were making me an apple pie. I'm not passing that up."

"Right this way, then." I took her hand and led her to my Jeep Wrangler, opening her door and waiting until she was seated and buckled before striding around to the driver's seat.

The orchard was located on the edge of town, and it didn't take long to get there. They gave us a bucket and showed us the apple varieties available for picking on a map.

"I think pretty much any apple works well for a pie," Luna said, swinging the bucket as we strode along a path beside the rows of apple trees. "What do you think?"

I took in the posts with tiny white lights strung between them. The moon had risen, and despite me being born wolf shifter and not a werewolf, the glowing orb called to me like it must've done to werewolves all those years ago.

"I can't believe you don't know that Macs make the best pies," I said with a laugh, taking her hand and squeezing it.

She pretended to gasp. "What makes you an apple pie expert?"

"As you kindly pointed out, I'm a prized chef. I even own my own restaurant." I said it with pride, not conceit. I'd worked hard for what I'd achieved.

"Why are you strolling through an orchard instead of cooking, then?"

"I have a fleet of chefs working at the restaurant, crafting dishes to my specifications. Now I mostly do managerial tasks." Which I actually liked. "But back to your sadly deficient take on apples and pie. Any old apple will not do. We want this pie to be perfect."

I loved pie. I couldn't wait to make—and eat—pie. But mostly, I just wanted to hang out with Luna.

She rolled her eyes. "Lead on, then, Mr. Pie Expert."

I pointed to a small sign, MacIntosh.

She darted along a grassy aisle between two rows of MacIntosh trees and stopped partway down to study the apples growing around us. They'd even strung twinkle lights between the rows, giving us enough light to see what we were doing. "Will these do?" Pointing, she approached a tree and, with the bucket on the ground, began picking.

"They're gorgeous. Would you like me to pick some higher up?" The tree was covered. It wouldn't take us long to fill our bucket.

"There's a ladder," she said, starting to drag it closer to the tree.

"Got it," I said, taking it from her and setting it up beneath the branches.

"Me first." With a laugh, she climbed.

I, naturally, followed all the way to the top where she

stood one step above mine. We weren't at eye-level, since I was six-eight to her . . . I'd say five-five, but we were close enough I could savor the humor shining in her eyes.

I tugged on a lock of her gorgeous blonde hair, loving the feel of the silky strands between my fingers.

"Hey," she said, swatting at my hand playfully. "We'll never collect enough apples for pie if you keep doing that."

"What if I do this?" I gently cupped her face.

Her humor fell, and her lips parted. Was there anything more inviting than that?

I leaned against her. "I'm going to kiss you, Luna."

"Stop talking and start kissing, then, Storm."

I claimed her mouth, and her kiss seared through me. I got lost in her fast, and the world around us ceased to exist. All I could think of was pleasing her, touching her.

She released a little moan and clung to my shoulders as if we were lost at sea and only I could save her. I'd protect her with my life; give everything to keep her from danger.

I lifted my head.

"Don't stop now," she said, tugging me close again. This time, she claimed my lips, and I was lost once again, drowning in the heady feeling of being with someone I . . .

I could love her. Only a twinge stabbed through my heart at the thought, followed by a mist of sadness that blew away in the wind.

When I was young, I had different plans, and they

were wrapped up in a friend who died. Life had a funny way of stealing someone away and then replenishing your empty well with someone new. It wasn't wrong to fall for Luna. It would be wrong to wallow in grief for the rest of my days.

We broke apart, and I pressed my forehead against hers, keeping my arms around her to make sure she was secure on the ladder.

"I like kissing you, Luna," I said.

"Same, Storm. Same." Her lips quirked up. "Let's pick the apples and make our pie, and then . . ."

"Then?"

"We'll see what else the night can bring."

CHAPTER 5

LUNA

We ran into Chastity and Max when we were carrying our bucket of apples up to the counter to pay.

"I'm so excited to get picking," Chastity said, shifting back and forth on her heels.

I'd seen her around town. She and Violet were best friends, though I hadn't had a chance to do more than casually chat with her. I'd heard a ton about Max from her, though. It was clear she adored her orc husband.

She grinned at Storm and extended the smile to include me, giving me a subtle wink. "I've been dying to sink my teeth into a crispy, tart apple for weeks now."

"I've been told pregnancy cravings stick around even after the baby is born," Max said, his arm around Chastity.

Their infant daughter slept in a sling strapped across Max's chest. I heard she'd had her baby early a few weeks ago.

"Congratulations," I said. I'd heard she delivered their baby two weeks ago.

"Thank you." Chastity stroked their daughter's dark-haired head. Her gaze fell on our bucket. "Max has been too busy to go apple picking. We both have been, actually." Smiling up at him, she leaned into his side, and he leaned over to kiss her forehead. "Max was just awarded a new job. You're looking at the general contractor of the new housing development going in on the south side of town."

"You won the bid?" Storm said, patting Max's shoulder. The guys were of equal height, though Storm was a little slimmer. But then, he was a shifter, not a burly orc. "Amazing."

"Goreg will handle the electrical." Pride showed on Max's green face. "I was going to give your restaurant a call to see if you'd like to handle our celebration dinner."

"How many people do you plan to invite?"

"Twenty, right sweetheart?" Max asked Chastity.

She nodded. "Twenty-two if you two would like to join us."

"Thanks. That's so nice of you," I gushed. This was why I'd hate to leave this town. Everyone was so welcoming. I felt like I'd finally found a true home here. I'd been looking for ways to get to know more people in Monsterville, and this would be the perfect chance.

The gleam in Chastity's eyes when she looked from me to Storm told me she thought we were a couple.

Were we? We'd done casual things this week, and

we'd just shared our first kiss, but we hadn't talked about further than that.

Did I want more? One hundred percent, yes. I liked him a lot.

The only thing that might drive a wedge between us was my past. Would I be given the time to develop a relationship with someone?

"I'd love to join your celebration," Storm said.

"Great. I'll be in touch," Max said. "It won't be for a few months, not until our daughter is older and Chastity has finished recovering."

"Give me a date, and I'll put you on the schedule," Storm said. "We can discuss the menu when it gets closer."

"Thanks," Max said. He lifted his empty bucket. "Apples await. My mate has a craving, and there isn't anything I'd rather do than satisfy it." He wiggled his thick unibrow at her.

"You," she said, poking his side. A wiggle of her finger, and he gave her a kiss that made envy soar through me.

What would it be like to be with someone who loved me as much as Max did Chastity? Actually, what would it be like to be with someone without my past shoving itself between us?

Maybe I'd find out with Storm.

We said goodbye, paid, and headed to the Jeep. Storm followed my directions to my tiny apartment and inside, we made the pie, him insisting on crafting the crust and innards with his own secret recipes. Once it had baked, we sat on my little, glassed-in back deck to eat big slices with scoops of vanilla ice cream melting on the side.

Then we gazed at the stars while the portable heater near our feet kept us from freezing. It would snow soon, and I couldn't wait to see it coat our cute town as if it had been dusted with confectionary sugar.

Monsterville was quaint and picturesque; they could film holiday romcoms here. I hoped I'd be able to stay here long enough to see snow fall through the sky. And spring! I couldn't imagine how it might look then.

Longing filled my heart to the point it might burst. Let's face it, I wanted to remain here forever.

"I'm always amazed by how close the stars look here," I said. "Like I could reach up and touch them."

"You should see how they look from up in the mountains."

"Gorgeous, I bet."

"Amazing."

"Maybe someday I'll rent a car and drive up there to see for myself." I didn't have a vehicle. I'd arrived here by bus and only with the clothing on my back and a big wad of cash. And while I had enough hidden cash to buy a car, I couldn't risk putting my real name on paperwork.

"I could take you up there sometime," Storm said.

I turned to face him. "I'd like that."

He swallowed hard. "I want to do lots of things with you, Luna."

Was this a good time to ask where he saw our relationship heading?

He leaned over and slanted his mouth across mine. Like at the orchard, heat flashed through my veins, centering in my core.

When I moaned and grasped his shoulders, he tugged me onto his lap. I wrapped my legs around him and deepened our kiss.

He traced his fingers down my arms and moved to my sides. Lifting his head, he watched my face as his hand slipped beneath my sweater. I wanted to tug it off, to toss it and my bra aside. My pants too. I wanted to be free to be his if only for one night.

Running all the time sucked; I never had a chance to build a friendship.

I never had the chance to fall in love.

He traced a fingertip along the edge of my bra, then glided it over my cloth-covered nipple. I leaned into his touch.

With a smile, he pulled his hand from under my sweater and tugged the soft knitted fabric down to my waist. "You're tempting. So much."

"So are you, Storm." I wanted to ask him to stay the night, but what we had felt sudden, though I felt like I'd known him forever. We fit together like pieces of a mosaic. Without each other, the pattern wouldn't be anywhere near as pretty.

He placed me on my feet and shot me a grin. "That's why I'm going to leave now. I'd like to see you again, though."

"I'd like that too."

I walked him out to his Jeep he'd parked in the space

allotted to me I never had use for. The apartment building only had three units; someone had turned an old Victorian into three cute homes, and the rent didn't overwhelm my budget. It might be noisy on the street sometimes, but at the price I paid, I couldn't complain.

He leaned against his vehicle and tugged me into his arms, turning me so my back faced him. His warm arms surrounded me, and I felt safe and warm, a fleeting thing for me for much too long.

His hand lifted, pointing. "Look, there's a satellite going by."

We watched as it soared past, a blaze of light in the sky.

"I have an odd question," he said softly by my ear.

I waited for him to speak.

"Would you be willing to come to my pack reunion with me this weekend?"

"It's Friday," I said with a laugh. "The weekend already started."

"Short notice, right?" He scratched the back of his neck. "Probably too short notice, huh?"

"Do you mean go with you as a date?"

"Yes. Or friends if that's what you prefer. We haven't talked about that, and maybe after one week, it's bold on my part to tell you that's where I'd love to see us going."

My heart twisted. He was handing me something precious, something I never thought could be mine. Did I dare risk holding on?

"It's hard to show up to these things without a plus one," he added. "My parents try to fix me up. My sister teases me about being undatable, and my cousins show off their mates and young. But I don't want you to feel obligated, however. Friends or a date or . . . Whatever you're open to is fine with me. We could even go as—"

"Storm."

"Yeah?"

"I'd love to go with you as your date." I could either grab onto what he offered and savor it for as long as it lasted or keep closing myself off to avoid being hurt. I couldn't say no to Storm, not like I had the few guys I'd gotten close to before I had to run once more.

Please, please, I prayed to the moon and the stars and whoever might be listening to the words of my soul. *Please don't make me leave him.*

"Okay. Awesome," he breathed, his arms tightening around me again.

That's when I noted a black sedan sitting on the opposite side of the street. Was it the same one I'd seen the other day? It couldn't be.

Please. No.

Like I starred in my very own horror film, and the inevitable was about to happen, the driver's side window slid down a few inches. I didn't see much more than a glimpse of his face, but his hawkish nose and clipped black hair were enough to bring my pulse to a shuddering halt.

One of my brother's henchmen had found me. Like every other time I'd fled, he'd been sent to track me down.

My pulse slammed in my ear, a discordant rhythm that scraped down my spine.

"You'll need to pack warm clothing," Storm said, unaware of how my heart raced and the chills shooting through me. "We'll be outside a lot."

"Alright." I gulped back a moan of despair.

The car started and pulled away from the curb, driving slowly down the road.

How could I stand here chatting when I should be grabbing my things and bolting?

Tears welled in my eyes, and I brushed them away.

The henchman wasn't leaving. He'd come back with reinforcements.

And my brother.

Running was my only option. If I didn't hide, they'd . . . I didn't want to think about what they'd done every other time they caught me. I could never let them catch me again.

Which meant I'd have to leave the little town I'd come to love.

And Storm, who I was beginning to love even more than the security I'd found here in Monsterville.

It wasn't fair. I'd just found someone . . . I pinched my eyes shut. I'd just found someone I could care for above all others. I didn't want to leave him.

I spun and clutched Storm's forearms. If only we were back in the ravine, hidden from the world, nestling close together. My favorite wolf would protect me from everyone.

Yet no one and nothing could protect me from what

was coming. It roared across the land like a thousand-foot tsunami.

"Is everything okay?" Storm asked, gazing down at me with concern. "You seem upset."

"Nope. Everything's fine." My words came out pinched. A glance over my shoulder told me the car hadn't returned, but it would before too long.

I would run, but . . . I needed this. Needed Storm, even if it was only for a short time.

I looked up at him, reading the caring in his eyes. Seeing such devotion there wrenched my heart sideways. "Can we leave right now?"

CHAPTER 6
STORM

I picked her up at her apartment in my Wrangler. Well, I met up with her in a lot two doors down from where she lived. While I was at home packing my bag, she texted stating she needed to get something from a store farther down the street, but I could swear there weren't any in that direction.

It didn't matter. I was thrilled that she wanted to come with me, that she wanted this to be a date.

When I parked in the lot and sounded my horn, she slunk out from behind a tall truck, peering around as if someone might be watching.

A quick scan with my wolf senses told me no one was. What was up?

She climbed into the passenger seat and tossed her bag in the back, buckling. Leaning back in the seat, she slunk low.

"Is everything all right?" I asked, puzzled.

"What do you mean?"

I kept thinking about the fear I swore shone in her eyes earlier, but I couldn't figure out why she'd be afraid. We were looking at the stars, talking about going to my pack reunion together. There wasn't anything scary about that. "You look like you're hiding."

"No, of course not. What makes you think that?"

The panic in her voice, for one. And the way her gaze darted everywhere as if seeking threats.

A growl ripped up my throat. "Is someone trying to hurt you?"

"Oh, nope. Not at all."

"Because I'll take them down. Rip their lungs out. Stomp them into the ground."

She shot me a look full of so much relief, it made me feel even more protective.

"I mean it," I added.

"Thank you. I'm okay. It's nothing." The smile she gave me didn't feel true. "Can we get going?"

If she didn't want to share or she wasn't ready to tell me what was going on, I'd let this go, though only for now. Since she appeared frightened about something, I'd remain on high alert. I'd eliminate any and all threats.

I drove from the lot, out onto the road, and took my vehicle through town, studying everyone we passed and the road behind me.

No one followed, but I couldn't shake off the feeling she needed help. Maybe it was just the jump-in-and-do-anything-for-a-friend thing I had going at all times. There wasn't anything I wouldn't do for Max, Goreg, Gunner, or their wives. We were pack, even if they weren't wolves. I naturally extended that to Luna, since it was clear we were becoming more than friends.

"Who's watching the dogs this weekend?" I asked, hoping to distract her.

"Violet said she'd do it for me." She eased up in her seat, still peering around, but she no longer clenched her hands on her lap. "She came by, and I showed her what to do. I only have Stella and Fred for the weekend, though, so they'll be easy for Violet to handle."

"I'm sure Goreg will help."

"He loves dogs as much as me. Funny how they're not a bit frightened of gargoyles."

"Dogs are smarter than people. They can tell who cares."

"That's right. Just so you know, I don't usually do anything like this. Go away and leave someone else to handle things. I take my job seriously. I want my clients to feel they can trust me."

"Everyone deserves a break every now and then."

"That's what it is." She shot me a smile. "A mini-vacation."

"This was short notice."

"Yes, that's it." She grabbed the excuse and ran with it. "At any other time, I'd defer taking in animals while I'm away."

"How many animals do you usually board?"

"Since there's only me running the show, I try to keep it to no more than four, though I'll make exceptions if someone really needs me."

"Have you thought of hiring staff?"

She sucked in a breath. "I couldn't do that to someone."

"It's a job."

"But I don't know if I'll have . . . enough work to keep someone employed. My grooming side of the business brings in the most revenue, so I try to focus my marketing there. I'm usually booked up all day."

"What about tomorrow? I assume you're open Saturdays."

"Oh, I rescheduled everyone for next week. I . . . needed to get away."

I was beginning to think whatever was going on here made her desperate to get out of town, though I couldn't imagine why. Monsterville might literally be overrun with monsters, but we all worked double time to make sure we didn't frighten the humans who'd give us their trust.

Monsters had stepped out of the woods and from below the ground three years ago, revealing themselves to humans. A treaty was formed, and now we lived among them. Most humans had adjusted quickly, though there were a few holdouts who periodically tried to mess things up. In Monsterville, we'd found a true home and acceptance, though that wasn't the town's original name. Blustery something. I couldn't remember, and it no longer mattered. To everyone, it had become Monsterville. There was talk of officially changing the town's name.

When we reached the edge of town, I turned onto the main road that would take us into the mountains.

"Want to put the top down?" I asked, trying to lighten the mood. I hated that something was bothering her, and I couldn't fix it.

"What?" she barked, her wide-eyed gaze meeting mine.

I waved to the soft top. "The roof," I said softly, gently, like she was a feral pup in need of a kind hand. "I can stop and put it down."

"Like, a convertible?" A cute frown formed on her brow. "It's barely above freezing."

"That just makes the experience invigorating."

"You're kidding me, right?" Laughter bubbled in her voice, and I loved that I'd put it there.

I shrugged. "Maybe. If you say yes, I'll be all over it." I'd be all over everything if she said yes.

I already had it bad for this lady. Could I persuade her to feel the same?

"You know what?" she said, sitting up straighter. "Let's do it. Put that top down, Storm. I want to feel the wind in my hair."

I pulled my vehicle to the side of the road, put it in neutral, and popped the emergency brake. "I suggest a hat, or your ears will freeze."

She grinned my way. "Maybe then I could get you to warm me up."

"Luna," My voice croaked. I wasn't sure how much teasing my heart could take.

Her smile wavered. "Too soon?"

"Luna," I said again. I cupped her pretty cheeks and kissed her nose, tempted to claim her ripe, pink mouth. I would soon, but not when cars passed us and while we were parked beside the road. Not when whatever she was afraid of could creep up on us while I was distracted. "You're a complete distraction."

"That's good, right?" she said merrily.

"Very good."

I popped the levers keeping the roof in place and undid the latches. Climbing out, I lifted the top, bringing it down to settle across the back, where I strapped it in place.

"Oh," she said when I sat beside her again. She hugged her belly. "It's really cold. I'm surprised we don't have snow yet."

"Soon. It's covering the tops of the mountains already." I tugged a thick blanket from the back and secured it around her, tucking it behind her shoulders and making sure it covered her from her jawline to her toes. Then I stuffed my red wool hat on her head.

I'd never seen anything sweeter than this woman encased in my things.

"That's much better," she said, giving me a smile sweet enough to crush me. "Onward!"

I buckled up again and steered the vehicle back onto the road. As I took us to the base of the hills and up into the mountains, I kept my speed low. While she welcomed the wind, I didn't want to turn her into a block of ice before we reached our destination.

"Are you okay?" I called out above the hum of my studded snow tires on the road and the wind whipping past us.

"It's wonderful!"

I wanted to kiss her pink cheeks and then find her mouth. I wouldn't pass up a second chance when it was offered.

"Tell me what to expect this weekend," she shouted.

"Pack reunion. Lots of wolf shifters."

"Will I be the only human?" I didn't find fear in her eyes; she was excited.

"Not the only one. Some have mated with humans."

"I wish I could shift into something other than me."

"It's wonderful."

"I could slip into the woods and disappear," she said forlornly.

Interesting way of putting it.

"Why do you want to disappear?" I asked.

"Oh, um, I don't. Not really." She kept her attention on the road. "Is your wolf side a separate person, or are you completely yourself inside when you shift?"

I paused, wanting to press this. How could I protect her if I didn't know what might be coming for us? And that was it. *Us.* Anyone after her wasn't coming just for her; I was beside her.

"I'll stand with you no matter what." I felt I had to say that.

Her warm gaze met mine. "Thank you."

"As for when I shift, the wolf you've met is all me inside."

"Cool."

"It's special," I said, appreciating the ability all over again. "Some might shrug it off, but I revel in being able to don a furry hide. Nothing can compare to the feel of snow beneath the pads of my feet, the wind ruffling my fur, and the pleasure I get from putting my nose to the ground as I run for miles."

"I can't imagine how awesome that would be."

I'd taken it for granted but seeing it through her eyes made me realize all over again how wonderful my shifter ability was. "Are you okay with the top down?"

She grinned. "Love it. Keep going!"

I turned my Jeep off the main road, onto a dirt track.

"Ohh, spooky," she said, peering at the dense woods around us. "I love it up here. You know I enjoy running in the woods."

I wanted to tell her to never run alone again, but how could I? She was her own person, and if a wolf knew anything, it was that you never put a collar on another.

"With the top down, I feel free, like when I run in the woods with nothing around me but chipmunks and birds. This is amazing." She shifted the blanket to the side and grabbed my hand where it sat on the shift, squeezing it. "Thank you."

"I'll take you for rides in my Jeep with the top down every day of the week if you want."

"Watch out. I might take you up on that offer."

Could my life feel more complete? Goreg was right; I should've talked with her sooner. But I'd finally stepped up and only the best awaited us.

I'd figure out what was frightening her, eliminate it, and nothing would hold us back after that.

"How much deeper into the woods are we traveling?" she asked in complete joy.

"We'll be there in twenty minutes or so." I downshifted to third until we'd crossed a rough stretch in the road, then popped it back up to fourth.

"Too much and never enough," she said.

"You're right." My heart felt completely full, yet I suspected there was room to stuff a few more good feelings inside before topping it off. I wanted those feelings to come from being with Luna.

We continued traveling, her gazing about raptly, me struggling to pay attention to the road and not stare at her all the time.

I felt like I stood on a ledge above the prettiest lake in the world. I wanted to jump off and splash into the cool wetness, but just as much, I didn't want to spoil the gorgeous, glassy surface.

Eventually, we reached the end of the road with the big clearing ahead.

"How many packs will be here this weekend?" she asked.

"Eight or ten, depending on who shows up. Ages ago, the packs built cabins all through this area. Each pack holds regular meet-ups here at different times, but every six years, we all join together. I haven't seen some of the other pack members in a long time." Including Marlie's pack.

"How many wolf shifters are there in a pack?"

"Thirty or so."

"That's a lot of wolves."

"Like you said. Too much and never enough."

"Oh, such cute cabins," she cried as I drove my vehicle along the path weaving around the outside of the huge clearing.

"Some packs come on foot, or pads, in their case, while others drive. A few pitch tents, some bring regular old campers, and the rest of us stay in the cabins. We hang out together, visiting all weekend. Alliances are renewed and fated mate connections are made." I'd planned to skip that part of the weekend; the moon ceremony would be held tonight.

"Ah, fated . . ." Her lips twisted, and I sensed her melancholy. "Wolfs mate for life, right?"

"We do. For some, this is their first chance to find someone from one of the packs to love."

"I didn't bring a tent," she said. Smiling, she shrugged. "But this is an adventure for me. I don't mind sleeping on the ground in the open air."

"It's too cold for that. We'll take cabins. You can sleep alone, or you can bunk with my younger sister."

Her gaze met mine, seeking. "What if I want to share with you?"

My lungs froze before joy shot through my chest, heating my heart up nicely. "Well, certainly. No pressure, of course." I pulled my vehicle into a space beneath evergreens and shut off the engine.

"Maybe I don't mind a little pressure." She turned back to watch as people stacked wood near the center of the clearing where we'd build a huge bonfire. "I've never been around an outdoor fire. I grew up in a city with concrete everywhere. I've been in Monsterville for three months, and I still can't get over all the vegetation around us."

"I couldn't live anywhere else."

Her eyes searched mine. "Nowhere else?"

While pack had always grounded me, I was beginning to think my home was where Luna placed her feet. It was too soon to say that, however. "I like it here." That was noncommittal.

"So do I. Monsterville is special. I can't imagine any place I'd rather live."

When I tugged off the blanket, she released a shiver. I grabbed my hoodie off the back seat and helped her put it on over her thick sweater.

"We set up heaters here and there to keep everyone nice and toasty, plus we'll have the fire, but we all bundle up. You'll see a lot of us in wolf form. Some don't shift into their human shape even once during the weekend."

"What about you?"

"When I'm with you, Luna, I kinda like being human."

"Storm." She swallowed, her gaze seeking my mouth.

I kissed her quickly, wanting to make it last forever, but others would come knocking on my car door soon, demanding I come visit.

"If you want to be a wolf this weekend," she said when we pull apart, "do it. I'll run with you in the woods or dance around the fire, whichever you prefer."

"You amaze me. So many people would be hesitant about sharing this weekend with us."

"They're afraid of shadows. I've learned to grab onto what I need most while it's within my grasp. Too often, I end up having to say goodbye."

There was a hidden meaning in her words. I was going to show her this weekend that she could trust me enough to tell me what was going on, to bare her heart.

I both wanted to rush what was forming between us but didn't. There was nothing wrong with savoring the feeling of being with someone new, someone who I was beginning to suspect could be the one.

These feelings weren't betraying Marlie. We'd been friends with potential we never had the chance to realize. She'd want me to be happy. Knowing that was freeing.

We got out, and Luna helped me put the top back up on my Jeep. With her bag in one hand and mine hooked over my shoulder, I took her hand and led her toward the clearing.

Mom called out when she saw me, rushing over to give me a kiss on the cheek. Dad followed, patting my shoulder before pulling me close for a big hug. They stepped back and studied Luna, Dad with a grin, and Mom with an inquisitive smile.

"Luna," I said. "Let me introduce you to my parents, Susan and John. Mom, Dad, this is Luna."

"It's nice to meet you," Luna said, her smile big and the shake of her hands almost as large.

"You came early," Mom said. "I didn't expect to see you until tomorrow."

I shrugged. "Couldn't stay away."

Mom stepped forward and gave Luna a hug. "Welcome."

Dad nodded, his grin at the same wattage as when he'd smiled at me. "Great to have you here for the pack meet-up."

"I'm not a shifter," Luna said.

"No problem," Dad said. "Neither was my mother."

"Ah." Luna's posture loosened. "I'd love to hear how your parents met."

"It's a fun story," he said. "Tonight, when we're lounging around the fire, I'll share it."

"Definitely," Luna said.

"Storm," someone called out. "Storm!"

Marlie's mom raced across the big meadow. She stopped in front of me, her excitement scenting the air. Her hair was grayer than I last remembered, but she was still the sweet lady I'd called a second mom. "There you are. So good to see you!"

"How are you doing, Fiona?" I asked. Marlie had looked just like her, and after Marlie died, it would make my heart pinch to see her mom at local pack meetings. That weight had lifted, and I welcomed the feeling that came from my growing affection for Luna.

Fiona's gaze drifted from Luna to our linked hands, and her face turned to stone.

"Who is this?" she barked.

Mom's concerned gaze met mine. Dad kept smiling like he hadn't picked up the sudden drop in temperature.

"This is Luna, Fiona," I said. "My . . . friend."

"She'll sleep in her own cabin or tent," Fiona said.

Dad grunted, his posture stiffening, but I held up my hand before he could speak.

"No, Fiona," I said. "She's sharing a cabin with me."

A blink, and Fiona shifted into her wolf form, her growl ripping through the air.

She sprung toward Luna.

CHAPTER 7

LUNA

As Fiona shifted and leapt toward me, a yip ripped up my throat.

Storm shifted into his glorious wolf form and leapt between me and Fiona, knocking her to the ground.

I wasn't sure why she'd attacked; I'd made no threats.

Susan grabbed my arm and pulled me away from the two wolves circling each other, their teeth bared and snarls rumbling in their chests.

Others peered in this direction. The concern on their faces told me it wasn't normal for wolves to fight at the reunion.

Fiona attacked, going for his throat. Storm ripped out with his claws, knocking her onto the grass. Smaller and leaner than him, she didn't stand a chance against a wolf in his prime. But that didn't slow her a bit. She scrambled to her feet and lunged toward him again, latching onto his back leg as if she'd hamstring him, then go for his jugular.

He rolled, striking out with his back claws, slicing into the side of her muzzle. She grunted and flung herself to the side, tumbling until she rose to her feet.

Storm shifted back into his human form and held up his hands. He stepped over to stand between me and her. "Fiona. Stop it. Don't do this."

"What's going on here?" someone said in a stern voice behind me.

A tall, muscular man with black hair graying at his temples and rich brown skin strode over to join us.

"This is George, president of this region's packs," Storm told me. "George, this is my date for the reunion, Luna."

I nodded in greeting.

"Nice name," George said before a scowl took over his face, directed at Fiona. "Shift," he snapped. "Explain."

As fast as she turned into a wolf, she became a woman again, stalking toward me and Storm.

George snarled, and she came to a halt. "I said explain." His voice might come out soft, but there was an edge to it that told me no one disobeyed this man.

"He's with *her*," Fiona said, her finger gouging toward me. Blood trickled from the slice Storm had delivered to her face with his back claws.

"Storm brought a date to the pack meet-up," George said. "He's not alone in that. We welcome everyone here."

"She's *human*."

"And in that, he's also not alone." George's gaze scanned the meadow. "I see humans, shifters, and even a gargoyle here for our reunion."

The gargoyle had his wings around a pretty woman with long chestnut hair. They appeared totally lost in each other. I'd seen him around town. Escudek? Yes, that was his name. Goreg's brother. I didn't recognize the woman.

"How could he do this to me?" Fiona cried, falling to her knees. "To Marlie?"

"Marlie has been dead for fourteen years," George said, though kindly. "Do you expect Storm to mourn her loss for the rest of his life?"

"*I* do," Fiona cried. "It feels like yesterday to me."

"For him, it was half his lifetime ago." George stepped over to her, placing his hand on her shoulder, squeezing it gently. "They were teenagers, not lovers or mates."

Marlie must've been Fiona's daughter. Had she also been Storm's teenage sweetheart?

He watched me with pleading in his eyes. I suspected he wanted to explain, and I'd let him. This weekend may be all we'd have. I wouldn't waste it by resenting someone he cared for before he met me.

"They could've been mates," Fiona said, cupping her face. She sobbed, calling her daughter's name.

"Marlie and Storm were best friends," Susan said, her gaze filled with sorrow. "Marlie died in an accident fourteen years ago."

Storm put his arm around my shoulders. "I'm sorry. I should've explained. I didn't think . . ."

How could he guess Marlie's mom would try to attack me? He must be shocked. If he and Marlie were good friends, Fiona must've cared for Storm too. It would hurt that she'd attacked, that she was upset to see him with anyone else.

George helped Fiona to her feet. "I'll take her to her family." His gaze landed on me and Storm. "Please don't think the packs feel the same. You are welcome here, Luna. This, I swear."

"Thank you," I said, my voice shaky.

"Let's go put our things in a cabin." Storm nodded to his parents. "We'll see you in a bit?"

"We'll save a place for you both at the fire," his father said.

They watched as George led Fiona away, her sobs making my heart twist into a tight ball.

Storm lifted our bags, and we walked along the row of cabins.

"Sorry about that," he said softly.

"I feel bad for her. It must be horrible to lose a child."

"Marlie and I . . ." He shook his head. "We were best friends. I always wondered if something more would've come from it, but we weren't given the chance."

"I understand."

He paused, watching my face. "She was special, but she would've wanted me to keep living, and I am. I hope . . ." He huffed. "It's probably too soon to say anything, but you're special, Luna." He stroked a strand of hair off my face. "I can't wait to see where this goes between us."

"Storm." Too much and not enough? Emotions nearly overwhelmed me. I wanted to experience everything.

He stepped back. "Anyway. I wanted to explain. I'm sorry it came about this way." After sucking in a breath and blowing it out, he started walking again, his voice lightening. "We'll take the first cabin without a smiley face in the front window."

"Smiley face?" The idea made *me* smile. It was a struggle to put aside what just happened. Finding a bit of humor helped. "That's cute."

He shrugged. "It works." His arm lifted. "There's one."

The last in this row. A copse of trees grew close to the cabin's right, and on the other side of the thick mess of trees, they'd built additional cabins. Others peppered the woods behind.

Shadows flitted through the forest, and I froze like a rabbit spotted by a coyote. If I ran, it would run me down.

Storm followed my gaze. "Packs are all over the place. No one else comes here during our weekend without us knowing from miles away."

He must've picked up on my fear. I hated bringing it between us.

It was reassuring to hear there were lots of people around, however. They'd notice if someone didn't belong.

When nothing moved in the woods, I swallowed, my spit clogging my throat. There was nothing worse than living with fear.

Inside the cabin, Storm turned on a light and flipped the sign in the window so the smiley face faced outward.

I took in the queen-sized bed, a small bedside table, a wooden chair, and a floor lamp. No bathroom, but I'd noted a big community building with signs along one edge of the clearing, plus a covered area with picnic tables beneath.

"We, um . . . Didn't discuss everything," Storm said, laying our bags on the chair.

I took his hand and tugged him close. In such a short time, he'd come to mean everything to me. I stroked the tendrils of hair hanging around his shoulders and huffed at the claw mark on his neck. "She hurt you."

"It's just a scratch." His intent gaze met mine. "I would never let anyone harm you. You know that, right? You can trust me to keep you safe."

"You've protected me from the first moment we met. I'll do the same."

But would I? If I was truly interested in protecting him, I would be on a bus headed for an unknown location, where I'd try to piece my life back together again. I wouldn't be risking him by stealing this weekend from fate.

My family had taken so much from me; I couldn't let them take Storm too.

He gathered me into his arms, lifting me up to meet

his mouth. I clung to his shoulders, knowing each time we kissed, it could be our last.

His mouth still moving over mine, he laid me on the bed and climbed over me.

My desperation took flight, and I tugged at his clothing.

He lifted his head. "I want you, but I need more time than we have right now. My parents will be banging on the door if I do everything I ache to do with you, because we won't emerge until the weekend is over."

"I want you too." A mournful cry edged into my voice.

"We have a few minutes, though," he said, his fingers tracing along my side.

I smiled and put my arms around his shoulders. "We should give things outside time to cool down."

"Exactly." He slid his hand beneath the layers covering my upper body, and a shiver of need tracked through me. "Would you like me to heat you up, Luna?"

CHAPTER 8
STORM

"I'm yours," she whispered, her voice hesitant and unsure.

Did she think I didn't want her? Or was she as afraid as I was of the feelings roaring through my veins?

"From the moment I met you, I wanted you," I said, my voice hoarse.

"You bolted the first time you saw me," she said, her voice dancing with laughter. "It gave me a complex."

I was standing on Goreg and Violet's front porch when Luna walked by with a dog on a leash. I should've approached her then, but spooked, I ran in the opposite direction.

"I felt like lightning shot through me when I saw you walking that dog past Goreg and Violet's B&B." I shrugged. "If it was today, I'd stride across the front lawn to meet you. I'd sweep you into my arms and kiss you."

"That might've startled me. Or maybe not. I feel like you and I have been waiting for each other forever."

"Fate has a way of sending people to each other when they need them most." My voice had gone husky.

I inched up her body, taking care since she was so much smaller than me, and kissed her again. She pushed up against me, moaning, and that was all I needed. I slid her outer layers up to find her skin.

She nudged me away, but only long enough to rip off my hoodie, her sweater and, sending me a coy smile, her bra.

Her breasts were round and would fit nicely in my hands. "You're gorgeous." So much more than I deserved. Life could take, but it could also give, and it had sent me this woman. I'd treasure her for as long as she remained in my life.

Easing my body downward, I swept the back of my hand along her stomach, my fingertips catching as they moved, then moved up and encircled her breast again, stroking my thumb across her nipple. She moaned again, urging me on.

I kissed across her belly to her breasts and sucked her nipple into my mouth. It formed a hard bud, and she lifted her chest up to my touch.

She dug her fingers into my shoulders, her eyes rolling back in her head.

"Storm," she said. "That feels so good."

I moved to her other breast, and she drew in a sharp breath when my tongue swirled across the peak.

"Don't stop," she gasped.

I kissed her again, framing her face in my hands, my tongue moving over hers as I teased her nipples with my fingertips, increasing the pressure and intensity. Lightly pinching them.

She groaned when I finally moved down her body again. I sucked on her stomach, causing her to writhe beneath me.

When I slid my fingertip beneath the waistband of her pants, she shucked her sneakers. She undid the top of her jeans and shimmied them down over her hips, kicking them aside. Beneath, she wore only pale lavender panties.

I nuzzled her through the silk and nipped the flesh of her hip bone, a small part of me wishing I could fly like Goreg so I could carry her all the way to the sea. I'd splash into the water and emerge, holding her. I'd kiss her. Make her laugh. Then I'd stroke her until she moaned my name.

Even racing through the woods in my wolf form paled when compared to being with her.

She eased her legs apart and closed her eyes, looking so beautiful and sensual my breath caught.

I shifted one of my fingers, revealing a claw and grinned up at her as I carefully sliced through the side of her panties.

She gasped. "Storm. I only brought a few other pairs." But the heady smile she fed me told me she wasn't upset I'd ruined the garment. "You," she chided.

"I'll buy you more. A thousand pairs."

She lifted her hips, and I tugged the scraps of her underwear from beneath her, tossing them to the floor.

Then I spread her legs and crawled between them, savoring how wet she was already.

When I extended my tongue to touch her, she cried out my name and arched against me, her hands searching for something to hang on to. She grabbed at the quilt, and I slid my hands under her ass, lifting her toward my mouth.

"Yes," she whispered, her eyelids closing.

I drew her clit into my mouth and sucked. Her hips shot off the bed, and she curled the fingers of her left hand in my hair. I pulled her into me, riding her body with my mouth and tongue.

"That feels so good," she whispered.

My claw gone, I slid a finger inside her, nearly coming at the feel of her wet inner walls sucking.

I continued to tug on her clit with my lips, alternating by swirling my tongue across it. It was a greedy bud, and I couldn't get enough of her taste and the sighs erupting from her throat.

She bucked beneath me; her cries going hoarse with need.

When I slid two fingers into her, she groaned.

"Yes. Yes, Storm. Like that."

Her tight passage clung to my fingers. My cock was a pole in my pants, and I couldn't wait to drive myself inside her, to ride her until she shrieked in ecstasy.

I could feel her coming undone, so I swirled my tongue over her clit, lightly grazing it with my teeth. I wanted to feel her come from my mouth and fingers alone. Later, when we could be alone all night, I'd claim her fully. I'd love her until morning.

She gripped my hair tighter, tugging on it, as she arched up to meet the furious strokes of my fingers inside her. Her inner walls quivered, and her clit swelled.

She cried out my name and her knees lifted, her heels digging into the mattress.

I continued to suck, riding the waves of her orgasm. She tipped her head back, and her cries reverberated around the room.

I nipped the inside of her thigh and flicked my tongue over her clit again, and she melted into the bed, her hands falling away from my hair.

When I eased up her body and kissed her, she must taste herself on my lips, her most intimate flesh on my mouth.

"Storm," she whispered, clinging to my shoulders. "What am I going to do with you?"

Love me, I hoped.

CHAPTER 9
LUNA

Storm lowered himself onto the bed beside me, his arms tugging me close. I laid on his chest until my breathing returned to normal.

What he'd just done for me . . .

I was no virgin, and a few guys had tried oral, but I'd never felt I could relax enough to enjoy it. With Storm, I felt like I could bare my soul to him, and he'd not only treasure it, but he'd also cup it in his palms and shield it with his life.

"I never thought . . ." I shook my head, unsure how to voice my thoughts or even if I should. Despite knowing I'd have to run soon; I didn't want to scare him away with heavy emotions.

He rolled me over until I was beneath him again and fed me a teasing smile. "I want to do that again. I want to sink into your warmth and love your body until it's hard to tell where you begin and I finish."

"That sounds amazing."

"A date later?"

My face heated. "Sure."

"I hate that we can't just stay here all night."

"I imagine your family wants us to join them at the bonfire," I said. "They must want to visit with you."

"Am I a naughty wolf for wanting to crawl all over you a few more times before we join them?"

"Not at all. I'd be happy to remain in this tiny, secure cabin forever." In Storm's arms, I felt safe. Nothing and no one could harm me.

"You'll have to feed me eventually," he said.

I snickered. "You just ate."

"That I did." He climbed off the bed and looked down at me. Should I feel vulnerable? I was naked while he was fully clothed.

Nah. I loved the heat in his eyes as he glided his eyes along my body.

When I licked my lips, he groaned.

"You're gonna kill me, Luna," he said in a growly voice. "I swear."

"What a way to go, huh?"

He held his hand out to me. "Let's go hang out. Do our duty to my parents and the packs. We'll escape as soon as we can, because there's nothing I want more than to be alone with you again."

I sat on the edge of the bed. "What sort of activities do you guys do during your pack meet-up?"

"The big wigs have meetings to discuss pack rules and policy, while the rest of us build the fire and enjoy it. Sometimes, we play games or hold official ceremonies."

"Will I be in the way for those?"

"Not at all."

"Do some play in wolf form?" I asked, standing. I shook my head at my torn panties. At least I'd brought more than I might need. I tugged new ones on, plus my lined jeans, topping them with a t-shirt, my sweater, and Storm's thick hooded sweatshirt that smelled like forest and him. Would he notice if I kept it after the weekend? When I ran, I'd need its reassurance and warmth.

My smile fell, but I turned away from him so he wouldn't notice.

How could I leave when I'd just met someone I could happily spend the rest of my days with? I wanted so much.

Too much and never enough was becoming my motto, but it felt like a curse when it came to me and Storm.

Could I hide in Monsterville? I'd only need to wait Vincent and his men out before they'd assume I'd left town. Then I could creep back out and be with Storm. Maybe I could talk him into living high in the mountains where no one would think to look for me.

Did I dare grab onto something I wanted more than anything?

If they caught me again, they'd make sure I never escaped. This could be my only chance to be with someone I loved.

Loved? I shook my head. I couldn't think of that right now.

"Are you okay?" Storm asked. He'd sat on the bed

while I dressed, the heat in his gaze making me want to peel my clothing off and drag him down on the surface again.

It would be wrong to endanger Storm and the packs. I had to trust Vincent hadn't followed us here. If he had, I would've seen him already.

If they knew where I was, they wouldn't waste time. They'd storm into the clearing and drag me away.

And Storm would not be able to stop them.

CHAPTER 10

STORM

"Hey, your friends are dancing around the fire," Luna said with a laugh as we strolled from the cabin toward the roaring blaze. "It's amazing."

When she paused, gazing in wonder at my pack, friends, and family, I stopped with her, putting my arm around her shoulders. She wore my sweatshirt and my hat, and I wanted to cover her in everything me. Sear myself into her so she'd never forget me. A primal, alpha wolf thought, but I couldn't help it.

She was mine. Pack. Friend.

And mate?

That I didn't know yet. After tonight, I might.

"It's so beautiful," she said, her eyes glistening with excitement.

Wolves danced around the huge bonfire, and even though I'd seen this many times while growing up, I was struck all over again by the majesty of my pack in wolf form.

I saw the wonder through Luna's eyes.

Flames illuminated their sleek, steel-gray fur-covered bodies, casting shadows that flickered across the ground. Their movements were graceful and fluid as they leapt and twisted, some passing over others who jumped up, nipping in play.

"It's breathtaking," she said. "I'm in awe."

Their yips and playful barks mixed with the crackling of the fire, creating a wild, primal melody that was both exciting and peaceful at the same time. It was pack. Me. Us.

And now, Luna.

My father raced toward us, shifting seamlessly into human form. His pace slowed, and he grinned at us both when he came to a stop.

"There you are," he said. "Your mother was about to send the hounds after you." His gaze flicked to Luna. "Are you hungry? Or do you want to join the dance?"

I looked to Luna.

"Dance," she said with complete joy. "Is it possible for a human to join in?"

He shrugged and glanced over his shoulder. "Storm's sister, Tayla, brought her gargoyle boyfriend, and there are other humans here, dancing. The more the merrier, I always say."

"Escudek, right?" Luna said. "I met him at my friend Violet's place. He's one of her husband's older brothers."

My dad's smile never slipped, and I loved him all over again, plus more. When he said anyone was welcome in our lives, he meant it. "Yes, Escudek. He's . . . wonderful.

Those wings! I can't imagine what it must be like to soar through the sky. And he's treating your sister right," he added to me. "I laid the claws on him the first time I met him. He's got a solid reputation in town, but I told him if he was playing with my daughter, the pack would be after him." He burst into laughter, though his gaze remained serious.

I was quite confident he'd spoken with Escudek, though I knew he hadn't made threats. No, that would come through loud and clear in his carefully chosen words.

"I'll lay claws on him too," I said, squinting toward the fire. Escudek lifted Tayla and flew high above the sparks, holding her close. I'd heard gargoyles enjoyed doing sexual things mid-flight. I doubted he'd try much while she was in wolf form, but she could change in an instant.

And when we shifted, it was clothing optional.

However, she was twenty-six, old enough to make her own decisions. Look at me, driving Luna to pleasure with my mouth not long ago. I wasn't one to talk.

"Let's dance," my father cried, shifting back to a wolf.

I took Luna's hand, and we raced after him. Mingling in with the others, we leapt and swayed around the fire, clinging to each other.

I kept stealing kisses. I couldn't help it. Kissing her—loving her—was my sole desire.

"Will you shift?" she asked.

"Would you like me to?" I ached to do it, because that

was when I felt most free, but I didn't want Luna feeling left out.

"I still keep thinking about you when you were a wolf," she said, swaying to the rhythmic tune played by a few guitarists. "You were gorgeous. I'd love to see you when I know it's you, Storm."

Who needed more incentive than that? I shifted quickly and nuzzled her fingers, licking them.

She stopped dancing and dropped to her knees.

I stepped into her arms, running my face across her neck, savoring her arms wrapped around me.

"It's amazing," she sighed into my fur. "You're beautiful."

I woofed. She was the beautiful one in this pairing.

Straightening, she started moving to the music again. The fire blazed behind her, shooting sparks into the sky as if fireflies danced with the packs. It was cold enough that her breath smoked the air. Her bright laugh as she spun and leapt made my heart sing.

I cavorted around her, dancing as only a wolf could, howling at the stars and the nearly full moon while racing toward the fire then back.

She spun, giggling, and tipped her head back, releasing her own howl.

Shifting back, I moved with Luna, our bodies rubbing together in complete harmony. The music sunk into my bones and drew out my primal heat. Wolf shifters had danced like this at pack gatherings for centuries. The meet-up wasn't just a chance to reconnect, but also an opportunity to create a better future for us all.

My parents scooted past us in wolf form, nuzzling each other's necks, and Tayla and Escudek gyrated not far away. I loved seeing everyone happy.

The song ended, and Luna and I stopped dancing, both of us panting. If I was still in wolf form, I'd claw at the ground in excitement.

My sister raced over, shifting into her human form as she reached us. The smile on her face made my chest ache. She was in love. I hoped Escudek would be kind to her. He swooped in and landed beside her, tucking a wing around her back. She leaned into him, gazing up at him in the same way I must look at Luna, as if she was my complete world.

Heat and affection lay in Escudek's eyes, and I was glad to see the latter. Since she was my sister, I didn't want to think about the first. But I assumed if she looked my way, she'd see the same expression on my face when I stared at Luna.

Escudek stood taller than all of us, the spikes on the top of his wing segments jutting toward the sky. His inky blue skin blended in with the night, his wings only a shade or two lighter than the rest of his leathery skin.

Until I met Goreg, I didn't know much about gargoyles other than that they remained within their flocks. Goreg was the black sheep of his family, as his wife Violet called him, because he'd left his flock and went to trade school, then started his own electrical business. The rest of the flocks extracted gems from deep beneath the ground and crafted them into exquisite jewelry and statues. They even smelted gold.

Escudek had remained with the flock, though he'd left long enough to help Goreg fix up the B&B where he now lived with Violet. How would my sister fit in with flock life? From the way they looked at each other, I suspected I'd find out.

"I'm Tayla, Storm's sister," she said, nodding to Luna. "I'm so happy to meet you. Mom and Dad told me you're amazing and that my big brother's totally smitten."

Luna grinned up at me, leaning into my side. "I'm humbled. Your parents are so nice."

"They're the best, right, Escudek?" She nuzzled his chest, and he encased her in his wings.

"They are," he said, his voice husky with emotion. "*You* are, Tayla."

"Hey everyone," George called out. "Guess what time it is?"

Excited voices echoed across the meadow, but they stilled at his words. Most shifted, and everyone moved around the fire to see what would happen next.

George jumped up on a wooden box, putting him a head above us all. "It's time for games!'

I took Luna's hand, squeezing it. "What do you think about scavenger hunts?"

LUNA

"Oh, a scavenger hunt sounds fun," I said, leaning into Storm's side. I'd danced with complete abandon, and for a few moments, I'd felt like pack, a wolf just like them. But as much as I thought it would be great to shift and run away, I enjoyed being human.

"Let's do it then." Storm urged me over to join those gathering around the leader, George. Fiona stood back from everyone else, watching. Her face remained neutral, but I felt the weight of her gaze. Her hands kept shifting to claws, and she flexed them into fists. I hoped she wouldn't make trouble.

"Some of you are new to the pack meet-up, so I'll explain the first game, a scavenger hunt," George said. "Yesterday, a few of us arrived early and hid small items throughout the woods, though all within three miles of the bonfire."

Tayla went around handing out small burlap bags,

smiling when she gave one to me. I nodded my thanks and looped the handle over my wrist.

"You get to keep whatever you find, but the person who brings back the most treasures will win a larger prize." His smile shot to Escudek, and he dangled a deep green stone on a chain in the air. "An emerald donated by the gargoyle flocks plus the gold chain it's strung on."

Ohhs and ahhs rang out as the stone spun. Firelight hit it, sending green beams arcing through the crowd like magic.

Escudek grinned, nodding to those thanking him for the donation. Tayla smiled up at him, her heart in her eyes.

"For the little ones, prizes are hidden close to the central area, so adults, I'm asking you to pace a quarter mile away before you begin seeking. To make it easier to identify which might be an adult scavenger hunt item and which are for the pups, those for the pups are wrapped in bright paper. Everything else has been placed in hidden locations, though I promise you won't have a hard time finding them."

One of the shifters in wolf form sniffed the ground, then tipped their head back and howled.

A bunch in human form laughed.

I leaned into Storm's side, and his arm went around me. "You guys are going to have it easy," I said with a smile. "You'll be able to pick up George's scent and follow it to where he hid the treasures. I'm going to have to rely on my eyes."

"Then you'll be happy to hear we compete in teams."

"You all have bags?" George asked, looking around. "The event is timed. You won't find everything, and that's part of the fun. You might find things left over from a prior pack meet-up."

"What sort of things are we looking for?" I asked.

Storm shrugged. "It could be almost anything. One year, I found peacock feathers and acorns painted with little faces."

Excitement rippled through me.

While the music had stopped, I was so happy, I kept dancing. "Thank you for bringing me."

"There isn't anyone I'd rather spend the pack meet-up with but you, Luna."

We kissed, and I wondered if we should disappear to our cabin instead of playing the game, but the whoops of the others sparked my enthusiasm. We'd be alone soon enough, and we'd share the cabin all night long.

My bones hummed as heat simmered deep within my core.

"Any questions?" George asked.

The silence was only broken by the buzz of anticipation in the air and the crackle of the fire behind us.

"One hour, then. Mark the time by the position of the moon, and when you're ready . . . Go!"

"Follow my wolf," Storm said, shifting into his wolf form.

I was grateful I wore running shoes, though it would be nice to be in full running gear. No matter. This was for fun, not exercise.

Stomps and laughter rang out around us as everyone swarmed toward the woods.

Storm bolted down a trail in the moonlit forest, stopping to sniff the ground then running again. When I gauged we were about a quarter mile away from the bonfire, I slowed my pace and started looking for hidden treasure.

"Ohhh," I sighed, spying something lovely at the base of a tree. I nudged aside a few raspberry stalks and picked up the tiny centaur. Carved of wood, it was about two inches tall. I stroked his tiny hooves and admired the simple carving that somehow made the person appear both majestic and mysterious at the same time. "Carvings, huh?"

"So far," Storm said from beside me. He took the tiny statue and turned it, looking it over. "Gorgeous work. A few of the packs have formed a guild. They sell their art at fairs and online. This looks like one of theirs." He flipped it over, pointing to the tiny paw print carved into the centaur's belly. "Yup, this is their mark."

I carefully placed it in the burlap sack.

"More," I said with a grin.

He bowed. "Your wish is my command." As a wolf, he took off down the path, though at a slower pace and with his nose to the ground. He darted to the left, shouldering aside young evergreen trees and mimicked a pointer by lifting his front paw, spiking his tail out straight, and nudging his nose toward another carving sitting on the top of a tree stump.

I scooped up the tiny carved troll, admiring the

sunny smile on his face and his slouched, pointy hat. He joined the centaur in our bag.

We continued down the trail, finding more carvings and even a few gemstones the packs must've purchased from the gargoyle flocks unless Escudek donated them too.

My favorite was the carving of a wolf who resembled Storm so much it brought tears to my eyes.

When I left, which I'd need to do soon, I'd take this carving with me. It hurt that it would be all I'd have of Storm, but what else could I do? I'd stolen this weekend to savor, but I couldn't ask anyone but myself to pay the price when it came due.

"Time," Storm finally said, peering up at the moon.

"How can you tell the time from the moon's position?"

He pressed his fist against his chest. "Even if my eyes were closed, I'd know in here." Coming around behind me, he placed his palms over my eyes. "Listen."

Crisp, cold air filled my lungs. The mountain breeze skipped through the forest, bringing with it the faint scent of pine and crushed fallen leaves. A few happy shouts mixed in with the faint click of branches in the wind.

"I don't hear anything," I said softly, not wanting to break the wonder around me.

"It's a whisper of something you can't define."

Letting complete calm fall through my bones, I held my breath. There. "It's like something wild and free swirling through the forest."

"That's her. The moon. Our wolf senses are so in tune with her, we can feel each slice of darkness gliding across her surface. That's how we tell time."

Amazing. I kept my eyes closed, leaning back into his warmth. I was in tune with nature, with Storm. My heart thrummed, and a glorious feeling rose inside me.

I felt more alive than I ever had, and it was because of him.

"It's wonderful here," I whispered. "I wish we could stay here forever."

"It's pack. The world around us. You and me, too, Luna." He held me for a long time. Eventually, he kissed the top of my head. "We should head back. But we can come into the mountains again, even to the meet-up spot when no one else is here. Before you know it, you'll be telling time by the feel of the moon too."

If only.

Sadly, I'd be long gone from here before that could happen.

We returned to the bonfire.

"Count your hoard," George called out.

Storm dropped to the ground and tugged me down onto his lap. We opened the bag and upended it.

"Eight," I said, showing him the carvings and jewels. "I have a feeling that's not going to be enough to win."

"We had fun, though, right?" he asked, his voice tickling my ear.

I nodded.

His arms tightened around me. "Then that's all that matters."

"Call out your numbers," George said, strolling around among us, pausing to admire the treasures we'd found. "Eleven. Fifteen!" he cried.

"Definitely didn't win," I said, though I didn't feel sad about it. Storm was right; if I was with him, winning a scavenger hunt didn't matter. I still got to keep the beautiful carved figurines and jewels.

"And the winner found eighteen," George called out from among the crowd. "I believe that may be a record! Tayla and Escudek will claim the prize."

Everyone cheered as Escudek hung the stone around Tayla's neck.

I leaned back in Storm's arms, stroking the tiny wolf carving.

"Since the pack meet-up is all about fun," George called out. "I hope this was a wonderful start to the event."

"Yes," I said with joy filling my heart. It might be silly, but I hugged the tiny statue.

"Wolves are special," Storm said softly.

I turned in his embrace and wrapped my arms around him, keeping a tight grip on my wolf. "You're special."

"Luna," he breathed, curling himself forward to reach my mouth.

We kissed until someone hooted.

"Save it for selection, you two," they called out, the words punctuated with good-natured laughter.

I pressed my face into Storm's chest, grinning. I felt

no shame in showing the world how much he meant to me.

"Are you hungry?" he asked, and I nodded.

We rose and strolled over to where they'd set up a buffet table beneath a wooden awning with open sides. The table held more food than an army could eat in a week.

I caught Fiona's eye as she stood further down in the buffet line. She snarled and stalked away, dumping her full plate in a bin as she passed. At least she wasn't attacking me.

After filling plates, we sat at one of the many picnic tables beneath the awning and ate quickly. Fresh air and activity had sparked my appetite, and I ate much more than usual.

"Would you like more?" Storm asked, laying his fork on his empty plate.

I shook my head. "That'll tide me over until morning."

"What about tonight?" he asked, super-charging the air with a new kind of tension. "Do you still have room for dessert?"

Flames licked across my bones, centering in my groin. I scooted closer to him on the bench, putting my arm around him. "What's on the dessert menu?"

"I believe there's a full buffet."

"Then I believe I'd like to—"

"Everyone," George called out behind us, reminding me we were still in full view. Although, I doubted many would care. If we made out, we wouldn't be the only ones. "Gather around again!"

"Want to see what comes next?" Storm asked, and I nodded.

We rose and put our plates in a tote and walked toward George.

"Do we need to help wash dishes or something?" I asked, peering back as a woman lifted the bin of dirty dishes and took it toward a building near the woods. "I feel a lot of work goes into making a pack meet-up run smoothly."

"I'm slated to work in the kitchen area tomorrow at noon and until dinner's over," he said, taking my hand. "If you want to help, you can be my sous chef."

"Maybe I want you to be *my* sous chef," I said playfully.

He kissed me quickly. "We can assist each other."

"If you'll come closer," George called out. "It's time for the next event!"

Storm put his arm around my waist as Tayla and Escudek joined us, watching George.

"Congratulations, winners," I said, admiring the stone dangling from her neck.

Tayla grinned, running her fingers across the smooth surface. "Thanks. Escudek's an amazing tracker. Flying, he was able to find more than I could even in wolf form and with my heightened sense of smell."

George climbed up onto his wooden box again.

"This is our most solemn activity," he said, nodding at the crowd in general. "Mate selection!"

Tayla's brow knit together, and she bit down hard on her lower lip before looking up at Escudek. "Yes?"

"Always," he said, his voice reverent and full of emotion.

The heartfelt way he said it made me suspect they'd already talked about this event but left the final decision to this moment.

Holding hands, they walked toward George, joining other wolfs and those shifted back to human form who were gathering around him.

"What's happening?" I asked Storm.

Storm stood behind me. He shifted my hair to the side and nuzzled my nape, his whispered words tingling across my skin. "Mate selection. We can watch."

I tilted my head back so I could see his face. "Do you want to participate?" Mate selection sounded . . . formal. Permanent? From the serious expressions on the faces of those around me, this was a momentous event.

"Nope. I don't."

Did he say that because there was no one here he wanted to mate with or because . . . "I assume I wouldn't be able to take part in it; it's for wolf shifters."

"As you can see, anyone can take part, even gargoyles." He nudged his chin to where everyone was forming a circle around George. "Look, there are a couple of humans joining the group too."

"Escudek looks nervous." The gargoyle shifted, and his wings kept fluttering outward.

"He's worried the moon will choose someone else for my sister than him."

"The moon chooses who they'll mate with? And when we say mate, do we mean sex or . . .?"

"Mating is for a lifetime."

"Like marriage."

"Without divorce."

"Never?" I asked, gnawing on my lower lip.

"If mates don't wish to remain together, they can part by declaring it to the moon."

"Does that happen often?" I asked.

"Rarely. The moon knows."

I already knew I wanted to be with Storm forever, but I worried my past would catch up and rip him away from me. I was terrified my brother would harm him.

"How does the moon decide?" I asked. Surely this was a ceremonial thing; the moon couldn't really choose a mate for someone.

Gasps rang out from the group, drawing my eye. The moon shone brightly in the clear night sky. Its light stabbed down, somehow finding a way through the bushy evergreen branches overhead. It softly caressed Tayla, then glided across the ground and lifted like a giant's flashlight to land on Escudek's chest.

His sigh bled out as if he'd been holding his breath.

George strode over to Tayla with a big smile. He took her hand and brought her to the center of the circle, then did the same with Escudek. There, he bound their wrists with a strip of leather. He lifted their joined hands, and everyone cheered.

"And so, my sister is mated to Escudek," Storm said, sounding as happy about it as me.

"It's beautiful." Tears welled in my eyes. It was a simple yet profound ceremony. "I never could've imagined anything like this."

We watched as the moon landed on someone else, then chose their partner. Three more couples were formed after that, joining Tayla and Escudek in the center of the clearing with their bound hands.

George looked up, as did those waiting. Clouds drifted over the moon.

"Ahhh," those waiting sighed as one.

"No mates for them?" I asked, taking in their sad faces.

"Not this time."

"Do they have to wait for the next big pack meeting?"

"The moon will shine again, be it tomorrow night or a month from now. It will find those who are destined to love each other for a lifetime and reveal their hearts to the world."

"I'm honored to share this," I said.

George went to each couple and kissed their foreheads, bestowing his blessing.

Tayla grinned up at Escudek, who looked vaguely stunned. But his wings remained around her, and the soft light in his eyes reflected wonder, not dismay. He must be as amazed about all this as me.

"What happens next?" I asked, thrilled to be a small part of the process.

"They run."

"Run?"

"Watch," he said with a smile. "Though I have a

feeling Tayla and Escudek are going to fly. Have you heard of the first flight? It's part of gargoyle mating tradition."

"I don't know much about gargoyles other than from the few times I've chatted with Goreg. He's a sweetie. He and Violet are happy together; he's completely devoted to her."

"When gargoyles mate, they consummate their marriage mid-flight."

"Wow." I watched as Tayla and Escudek hugged the other couples. Those not chosen by the moon went to get something to eat, and a few joined those adding wood to the fire.

Tayla and Escudek left the group and, holding hands, strolled into the woods.

"I don't believe we'll see them again for some time," Storm said.

"The other couples won't be flying."

"And that's where the run comes in," he said. "The moon chose, but now they have to decide if their wolves agree."

The other couples released their wrist bindings. They shifted and their partners remained on the edge of the woods while the first group raced into the darkness. A few seconds later, the second group of wolves took off after the first.

"I'm not sure what's happening," I said.

"They run. They're caught. And if their wolves agree, they shift back and . . ."

"Ah." I chuckled. "Sounds kind of sexy."

"It's primal. A tradition as old as wolf shifters."

Something inside me told me to run, to let Storm catch me. I could picture us entwined, giving into our needs with only the forest around us.

I looked up at him. "What would you do if *I* ran?" A thrill shot through me, and I knew this was it.

Why wait to claim my dessert once we were inside the cabin? Being alone and out here in the wild with him brought out a need I could barely define. It made me crave him in a way I'd never wanted anyone else.

A growl of need rumbled in his chest. "Why don't you run, Luna, and find out what happens?"

"Maybe I will." With a husky laugh, I slipped from his arms.

I jogged toward the woods with my hair streaming behind me and my heart on fire.

When I hit a path, I kept going.

The pads of Storm's paws thundered behind me.

CHAPTER 12

STORM

After tossing me a lusty glance, Luna had bolted into the woods, embracing pack tradition. My blood roared. She was calling for a mate to hunt her down and claim her.

Heat boiled within me, tempered by the cool, welcome light of the moon.

I shifted and raced after her, my heart thundering.

Just as my ancestors had done before me, I hunted the female I wanted above all others. When I caught her, I'd make her mine. Whispers suggested claimings could be wild, untamed ruttings, but no one would take a female without their consent. That was sacred among my people.

Being moon chosen was a revered thing to be honored and cherished, and the solidifying of the bond that followed was treasured above all other things.

I remained behind Luna, giving her a chance to put

some distance between us and the others. Her laughter rang out, and I savored the sound of her joy. When I caught her, I'd kiss her until she moaned. And then I'd show her how much she meant to me.

She hit a long stretch in the path and picked up her speed, bursting out into a small meadow. Her pace slowed in the deep grass, and I easily caught up. Few could outrun a wolf.

But it was clear she wanted to be captured.

I pounced, shifting mid-air. Grabbing her, I took us down, holding her close to take the brunt of the fall with my body.

We landed in the grass, and I rolled, finally coming to a stop with her lying across my chest. She braced herself over me. Her smile warmed me through. Her fingers on my shoulders sunk into me like melted honey. And the heady light in her eyes sparked heat deep within me.

Seeing her like this made my heart ache.

Moonlight stabbed down from above, gliding across her gorgeous features.

Her gasp rang out as she looked up, her face filling with wonder.

The moon danced across her, making her skin sparkle, before it landed on me, doing the same. A wink and it was gone.

"We . . ." Her gaze met mine. "Storm. This means we're . . ."

"Moon chosen."

Awe filled me. This was why I'd fallen so fast for her,

why I'd been unable to stay away from the moment I saw her. My heart knew already. My brain just needed time to catch up.

"Storm," she said, tears trickling down her cheeks.

I wanted her to be happy, but it appeared being linked to me wasn't doing that for her.

"You don't want me." Pain stabbed through my chest. It was all I could do to breathe.

"I do."

I wasn't sure why, but I sensed desperation rising inside her.

"Claim me, mate," she said. "Make me forget the world. Give me a memory I can . . ." She pinched her eyes shut, and when she opened them, only happiness filled her gaze. "I want you."

There was more going on here than she was admitting, but I'd never force her to share. She'd do so when the time was right.

"Love me, Storm," she whispered. "That's all I need."

I did love her, and I would forever.

Her mouth sought mine, and I didn't need anything more than that.

I rolled until she was beneath me. As we kissed, our breathing grew ragged. We tugged at each other's clothing, removing each item with small bursts of laughter when an arm or leg got stuck in the fabric. Our heady sighs rang out as we stroked each other.

The heat growing between us pushed aside the chilly air.

I traced my palms up her sides, teasing her skin and

finding her breasts, cupping them. When I ran my thumb across her nipple, she moaned and thrust up to meet my touch.

One of her hands pushed through my hair, holding me close. The other slid over my neck, my throat, and my chest, teasing my nipples while I did the same to hers.

My cock was a solid rod between my legs, and anticipation kept jolting through me. Soon, I'd be with her completely. It would be all I could do not to cum right away. It was important that she was not only with me, but that she enjoyed it even more than me.

When she pinched my nipples and rolled them between her fingertips, I growled against her mouth. I kissed along her jaw and down her neck, moving my body lower to reach her gorgeous breasts. I needed to taste them more than I needed to breathe.

My hand moved of its own accord, sliding down her body and between her thighs.

She opened herself to me, spreading her legs wide, and I groaned when I felt how wet she was already. Gliding my fingers up her seam, I found her clit while sucking one of her nipples into my mouth.

She bucked beneath me, her hips straining upward while she arched her spine.

"I need you," she gasped out.

"I'm yours, mate," I said reverently. Some wolves waited their entire lives without being moon chosen. I'd been given an incredible gift, and I would thank the moon for the rest of my days while loving Luna.

I thrust two fingers inside her. She was tight, almost

too tight. For a moment, I worried that I wouldn't be able to fit, but as I pushed my fingers deeper, her muscles relaxed. She sighed and her eyelids fluttered closed. She clung to my shoulders.

Her eyes opened again, and this time, I couldn't breathe as I looked into them. Even without words, I could tell the same reverence filled her.

It humbled me, and I loved her even more.

I ran my tongue across her nipple while thrusting my fingers inside her. I added a third, and she was so damn snug I nearly came.

Her eyes closed again and bit her lower lip, exposing the delicate column of her neck to me. I moved up her body and kissed where her pulse thrummed, knowing it would be a sensitive spot, and her breathing hitched. She was so responsive. Her hand clenched my shoulder, but she relaxed, spreading her legs wider. As I kissed lower, across her belly, she clung to my hair.

Her pretty little clit glistened in the moonlight. I had to taste it.

While moving my fingers within her, I sucked her clit into my mouth and ran my tongue across it.

She moaned and curled her fingers through my hair, holding tight.

With each stroke of my tongue, I licked and sucked up her glorious juices. Her moans grew deeper, hoarser. Her thighs clung to the sides of my head as I licked down her slit, pushing my tongue inside her along with my fingers.

"Storm," she whispered, her head thrashing in the soft grass.

I loved how she trusted me completely to make sure she found pleasure.

Finding her clit again with my tongue, I focused on the tight circle of muscles around my fingers as I pushed them deeper.

Her hand gripped my hair tighter. "Don't stop. Never stop."

I rocked my fingers within her, my tongue still focused on her clit. One of her hands released my hair, and she slid it to my shoulder. She clung to me, her body tightening beneath mine.

Twisting my fingers, I made sure I hit her G-spot.

And when I sucked hard on her clit, she came with a scream. She rode my mouth, bucking up while her guttural cries echoed in the small meadow.

"Yes," she moaned. "Storm. Yes."

She continued to rock against me, her breathing ragged as her body continued to shudder.

I kissed up her body, pulling my fingers from her wet sheath.

She reached for me, her hands sliding up my sides.

"I love you," she whispered.

Ah. I'd never been so honored. "I love you too." I didn't care that my voice was hoarse or that I handed her everything inside me by speaking the words.

She was the world, the stars, and the moon to me.

"Take me."

"You're sure?" I said, still remembering how tight she was. How big I was.

She gave me a grin and nodded. " I'm yours."

She watched as I hitched her heels up onto my shoulders.

I centered my throbbing cock at her core and thrust forward, burying my length inside her.

CHAPTER 13

LUNA

He was big and thick, and he was all mine.

The second he was buried to the hilt inside me, I could feel my body starting to twist tight all over again. He'd just given me a powerful orgasm, but I sensed before he was finished with me, I'd come at least once more. The second time was going to be even better than the first.

"Luna," he groaned as he pulled out and pushed back inside. He rocked against me, alternating his pace as I rose to meet him.

I worried I'd explode too soon. I needed to feel him coming along with me.

"You're gorgeous. Wonderful," he said. "I can't get enough."

I clung to his shoulders as he picked up the pace.

"You're with me?" he growled.

"Yes. More, Storm. More."

While my soft cries of joy echoed around us, he moved faster, his body slamming against mine.

"I want to crawl inside you and stay there forever," he said. He glided his fingers down across my hip and found my clit, rolling it.

"Storm. Yes," I hissed. "Like that." A whimper slipped from me.

He continued to push himself inside me, and his body tensed.

"Come," I said. "I'm with you." Always with him.

His muscles tightened, and his hoarse groan rang out.

We came together, loudly, explosively, a meeting of his world and mine, one that would remain with us forever. His hot seed bathed my inner walls, driving me to come again. I was wracked with one orgasm after another until I felt like I couldn't take any more.

With a growl, he curled forward and nibbled on my shoulder. He bit down hard enough to leave a mark, though not breaking the skin. The sensation felt amazing.

"You," he said.

"You," I echoed, unable to stop grinning. "I feel wonderful."

"*You're* wonderful. Amazing. I'll never be able to get enough of you."

His arms slid around me, and he rolled until I lay on top of him. "You've heard of knotting, correct?"

I frowned. "Only vaguely and related to . . ." Oh, dogs.

Ha. "You do feel bigger down there." Thicker, too, as if he'd expanded even more.

His cock twitched, pushing deeper. The sensation triggered delicious quivers deep within my core.

"How long will we remain locked together?" I asked, loving how wonderful this felt.

Loving him.

"Not long enough." His arms tightened around me, and I sent a wish to the moon.

Please don't make me leave him.

CHAPTER 14

STORM

We returned to the central pack area and devoured platefuls of snacks beneath the awning.

Other newly paired couples trickled from the woods, joining us. We chatted, laughed, and pure satisfaction filled the air.

Escudek landed in the clearing, holding my sister. Holding hands, they walked over to the snack buffet.

The look of intense happiness on Tayla's face made me stride over to Escudek, bringing Luna with me. The women hugged, laughing with joy while I shook Escudek's hand. And because I was so full of happiness myself, I hugged him, patting his . . . well, I couldn't reach his back, so I patted his wing tucked against his spine.

"Welcome to the family," I said as I stepped back.

"Thank you." He beamed at Tayla, tucking her close to his side.

They grabbed plates. I turned to Luna.

"Would you like to dance around the fire some more?" Taking her hands, I squeezed them. I wanted to hold her forever, but I supposed I'd have to release her at one time or another.

"Let's go to our cabin." The soft smile she gave me made my heart pound. Just like that, I wanted her again.

We washed up in the his and hers bathrooms, then went to our cabin, stripping and climbing into the bed.

Luna was shivering until I tugged her close, wrapping her up in my arms and my warmth. We started kissing, stroking each other, and soon, we were both moaning wrecks.

Rolling her onto her back, I spread her legs and crawled down between them. I'd never get enough of pleasuring her. I didn't even care if I came myself. Her satisfaction meant everything.

I licked up her slit, stabbing my tongue inside her when I passed, then focused on her clit. It was cute, engorged, and all mine.

Luna's body quaked in response, her fingers grasping my hair as I drove her body ever higher.

I continued to tease and tantalize, feasting on her sweet wetness until she had turned into a writhing, whimpering wreck.

Nothing could make me happier than this. Just being with her. Loving her. My entire reason for existing was to please my mate, to pleasure her every night for the rest of our lives.

I moved up, kissing the length of her body and savoring her cries of joy.

When I reached her breasts, I stopped and sucked one of her nipples into my mouth, rolling it while she thrust her chest up to me. I continued to suck while stroking her other breast, teasing that nipple into a hard nub.

I rolled her over and lifted her hips, grinning at how wet she was, how her lips parted for me.

She thrust back toward me. "I need you, Storm. Please."

How could I resist her?

I lined my cock up against her entrance, teasing her by gliding the thick head just inside, then pulling back out. When she whimpered and fisted the covers, shoving back to meet each of my short thrusts, I couldn't hold myself from claiming her any longer. I drove my cock inside her, growling in pleasure as her tight walls surround me. Luna gasped and moved her hips in a slow rocking motion that had us both moaning in delight.

Relaxing into each other, I began to thrust with slow strokes, gradually increasing the speed as she moved back to meet me.

I leaned over her and stroked her clit, savoring how she quivered and sighed when I did it.

She gasped, and her body started shuddering as she gave into her first climax.

My movements became frantic and passionate as our lovemaking intensified. With every thrust, my breathing quickened, and my heart beat faster. The passion between us was palpable, a thick cord binding us to each other. It could never be severed.

I reached my peak at the same time as her, crying out her name. My cock thickened and the head swelled as I moved within her, claiming everything her body gave and giving it back over and over.

With my cock knotted inside her, I held her, easing us down onto the bed still linked. Pure bliss filled my heart, my body, my soul.

"I don't know how I ever survived without you, Luna," I whispered, stroking her body. When I ran my fingers across her breast, pausing at the sweet bud of her nipple, her inner walls quivered around me, making my cock pulsate once more.

When my cock finally unknotted, I pulled out of her and turned her so she could lie on top of me.

She stroked my chest as I tugged the covers up over us.

Then I held her.

I didn't release her, not as the moon slowly hitched toward the horizon or even as dawn's bright light bloomed in the sky. I kissed the top of her head as she slept, and I sheltered her in my arms.

Only when I heard those assigned to cook our breakfast moving around outside did I finally sleep.

Though I took it, I didn't need rest.

Holding my mate in my arms rejuvenated me.

CHAPTER 15

LUNA

I woke lying across Storm's chest.

He stroked my back, and I vaguely remembered him doing the same thing, plus kissing my head and holding me all night long.

"Did you sleep?" I whispered.

"Enough."

Maybe we could take a nap later. Although that might not generate much sleep either.

"I'm going to the bathroom." Sliding from the bed, I tugged on my jeans and a t-shirt, stuffing my feet into my sneakers. I topped the outfit with Storm's sweatshirt that I was never giving back.

He watched me with a heady gleam in his gorgeous green eyes. It made my heart skip a beat. "Come back?"

The eagerness in his voice was enough to make me hurry but seeing his cock stiffening made me grin.

"Sleep," I said, trailing a finger across his chest. "I'll wake you when I get back."

"You think this thing will let me sleep?" He tapped his bobbing cock.

"Yeah, hold that thought then."

I grabbed my bathroom kit, a towel, and a change of clothing, figuring I might as well shower while I was there. Despite my eagerness to ride his cock, I wanted to give him time to rest. It felt wonderful to sleep in his arms; I'd felt safe for the first time in forever. But he needed rest too.

After showering, I stepped outside the cabin.

Hearing what sounded like crying, I started looking around. Was there a wounded animal nearby?

Close to the back of the building, I found a boy about five-years-old sitting inside a stone-sided hole. Why someone had dug a hole in this location was beyond me, but my biggest worry was for the boy.

"Are you okay?" I asked, kneeling on the edge of the hole that looked about eight feet deep.

"Me and Toof fell down," the boy said, looking up at me. He scrambled to his feet.

"Are you okay?" I asked softly.

He nodded. Tears streaked his face, and a small bruise was forming on his left temple. Other than that, though, he appeared unhurt.

"Toof is you friend?" I took in the Chihuahua sitting beside him, looking up at me with puppy hope in its eyes.

"Toof fall," the boy said. "I had to help him!"

"I'm sure you did." I sat and dangled my legs inside

the hole. "I'm going to come down with you. Move back so I can jump, okay?"

"Okay." The boy picked up the puppy and backed to the other side of the six-foot-wide pit in the ground.

I leapt, landing squarely, and stooped, holding out my arms toward the boy.

He rushed to me, and I held him, patting his back and murmuring nonsense words to reassure him. When he'd stopped crying, I sat and held him some more, stroking his hair while the puppy licked his face and tried to leap up to get to mine.

"Trevor," someone called out from the front of the building. "Where are you?"

"Are you Trevor?" I asked, and he nodded. "Then it looks like someone's looking for you. Your mom, maybe?"

He shook his head. "Auntie."

"Then your auntie." I stood, holding him. "Here. We're here!"

"Trevor?" The voice grew louder.

"Here," I cried. "I've got Trevor here! You'll have to help us."

Footsteps approached, hurrying along the side of the building, and Fiona stooped down beside the hole, peering at us.

Ah, Auntie Fiona, I presumed.

"What are you doing with my great-nephew?" she spit out.

"I fell, Auntie," Trevor said, wiggling in my arms.

"I heard him crying and investigated," I said. "I found

him here with his pup. I'm not sure why there's a hole so close to the main area, but you guys should fill it in before someone else gets hurt."

"It's a bulkhead."

What a place for a bulkhead. I took in the stone sides and a wooden hatch I'd missed on the back wall. "Maybe they should improve it a bit? Stairs would come in handy, and if they covered it, no one would fall inside."

She peered around. "They're still working on it. They've been covering it with a piece of plywood to keep out water and prevent things like this from happening." She pointed to the hatch. "That's an emergency exit from the basement. I don't know where the ladder or the cover went, however."

I eased Trevor off my lap and stood. "I'll hand him and his pup up to you."

Her lips tightened. "Thank you."

I imagined it was hard for her to say that to me. "You're welcome. I felt bad for him. He seems to have bumped his forehead. We should get that checked out. But other than that, he doesn't appear to be hurt." I put him down. "Grab Toof and I'll give both of you an elevator ride to the top."

"Ev-ator?" he asked, his brow scrunching. "What's dat?"

"You'll see." I smiled to reassure him. "Are you ready for your ride?"

"I am." He clung to Toof and hopped in place. "Want ev-ator ride!"

"Coming right up," I said cheerfully. "Put your arms

up to Auntie." I lifted them, and she grabbed onto him, tugging him the rest of the way out of the bulkhead.

Fiona placed Trevor on the ground and looked down at me. "The ladder's leaning against the back wall. I'll lower it down to you."

I almost expected her to leave me here. That would take care of what she saw as a problem. But she did as she said, carefully placing the metal ladder into the hole.

She watched me climb out, a frown knitting her face. "Thank you again. Trevor's a sweetie but rather mischievous."

I shook my head. "Like most pups, right?"

"Yes, like most pups." She turned and took Trevor's hand. "Let's get you to your mother, honey. She's been looking for you everywhere." She led him to the side of the building, shooting me a look I couldn't define before taking the boy toward the central meet-up area.

I brushed off my jeans and grabbed my bathroom bag off the ground, slinging it over my shoulder.

My steps were lighter as I returned to our cabin.

Maybe Fiona didn't hate me any longer.

CHAPTER 16
STORM

After breakfast, we helped carry firewood and kindling for tonight's fire from the shed built a short distance away. Each summer, I came here with others to cut wood from the surrounding pack land and split and stack it inside the building.

"What's on the agenda today?" Luna asked. She kept shooting glances Fiona's way. Had the other woman said something horrible to Luna? Irritation rose inside me, followed by an urge to rip people apart to protect my mate. Part of this came from our moon-gifted bond, the rest from pure love.

"Is everything alright?" I asked.

I wanted to glare at Fiona, but my heart softened whenever I looked at her. She'd been like a mother to me while I was growing up, and a friend since. A mix of feelings churned inside me. I'd do anything to protect Luna from her, but I wished there was a way Fiona could see how much I cared for Luna, that she'd accept that I was going to be with her.

If anything, however, Fiona's expression was confused, not angry. Maybe she was coming to see the Luna I'd fallen in love with.

"Yes, it's fine," Luna said.

"Look, Luna!" Trevor, Fiona's great-nephew came running over to us. "Look! I gots you a flower." He gave her a huge smile. "I pick it myself."

"Oh, my, it's gorgeous," Luna said, stooping down to the boy's level and taking the stalk of goldenrod from her.

Trevor's chihuahua scampered over to join us, jumping up on Luna's knee.

"And how are you, Toof?" Luna asked, ruffling the little pet's back while it wiggled with joy.

"He can't talk," Trevor said in complete seriousness. "He's a dog, not a shifter like me."

"I guess you'll have to talk for him, then, right?" Luna straightened and smoothed the boy's hair, glancing my way. "I need to tell you about the adventure me and Trevor had this morning."

"She rescued my great-nephew," Fiona said, joining us. "And I am eternally grateful."

"Oh, I didn't do anything like that," Luna said. "He'd fallen into the bulkhead hole behind the bathroom building, and I climbed down and gave him a boost out."

"I am still appreciative," Fiona said stiffly. Her gaze traveled down Luna's front, but her eyes no longer held malice. She sniffed and took the boy's hand. "Come along, Trevor." Her attention fell on us as she turned away. "I swear. Your mother needs to put a leash on you, not Toof."

I tugged Luna into my arms. "You're amazing, you know that."

She grinned and squeezed me right back. "I had other things on my mind when I got back to the cabin, or I would've mentioned it." She tugged my head down and kissed me.

In no time, I was wrapped up in her, oblivious to everything around me. In fact, we needed to go to our cabin and—

"Now, now," George said, strolling past us.

We broke apart, chuckling.

"Pups are around," he said with a grin. "Save the moon chosen stuff for later. From what I remember from the schedule, you two are slated for kitchen duty for lunch and dinner anyway. That should keep you busy."

She and I looked at each other and burst into laughter.

"We're on it, boss," I told George, taking her hand.

We strode over to the big building where we held community gatherings when it rained. On one side, we'd installed a kitchen where our meals were prepared. The head of the kitchen gave us assignments, me making cookies and Luna chopping vegetables. My fellow shifters sang or hummed softly as they worked, and I soon joined in, harmonizing with whatever tune they chose.

Luna kept shooting me grins and it wasn't long

before she was humming and hip bumping me whenever she passed.

I loved how she fit in with the packs and even more, I loved seeing her smile.

Even Fiona wasn't shooting daggers our way any longer. Sure, she still held herself back, but when she glanced Luna's way, she didn't look poised to attack. Given time, she might even become friendly. Too bad there wasn't time for that to happen during this gathering.

We worked in the kitchen area through the afternoon and early evening. After the dinner hour, someone else took our spots in the kitchen, starting in on the huge piles of dishes. We helped build the fire, and it soon crackled, sending light dancing around the meadow. The sun had nearly set, and cool darkness would soon claim the world.

I couldn't wait to be alone with Luna again. Could I talk about us moving in together during our ride back to town? It might be rushing things, so I'd sound her out first. I'd make arrangements to see her as much as possible this coming week and see where things went from there.

We stood holding hands with the flames behind us. Mom and Dad stood nearby, Dad nodding Luna's way in approval.

"If you'll all gather round," George announced. "We have another game to play!"

A few kids scampered over to peer up at him, clambering for him to share.

"Not you, kiddos," he said with a smile. "This game is for adults only."

A chorus of disappointed moans rang out, but one of the moms lifted a horn and blew it, making silence descend.

"Who wants their face painted?" she called out, and the kids abandoned George like a week-old bagel.

"Are you up for a game?" I asked Luna.

Biting her lower lip, she darted a glance at the surrounding woods and nodded.

I cast out with my wolf senses, but I didn't find anything near other than forest creatures. A bear lumbered along a deer trail five or so miles away, but he wouldn't come close. Why did she seem to feel threatened?

"Tonight, we're going to play hide and seek with a twist," George said. "A friendly twist, please."

"Ohh," Tayla said, leaning into Escudek's side. Whenever I'd seen them today, his wings were around her and they were gazing at each other with complete love. I was happy for them and hoped every day of their lives would be filled with joy.

"We'll divide our group into two teams and split the humans and our gargoyle friend among both teams to make it fair." George held up a small basket. "If you'd like to play, pick a ribbon. Those who choose blue will be on team one and yellow will make up team two. Tie the ribbons around your upper arms."

We got in line behind the others, slowly weaving toward George as he continued to lay out the rules.

"The blue team will be given ten minutes to hide, and then the yellow team will seek them. The yellow team has another ten minutes to locate as many blue team members as they can and tag them." He held up red ribbons. "Just tie one of these—loosely, please—around each person's arm after you track them down, then send them back here. Once the first round is finished, the yellow team will get their chance to hide. When both teams have finished, we'll add up the tags and the team with the most catches wins."

"Yellow," Luna said with a smile, waving the ribbon my way.

I held up blue, and her smile faded.

"You're not upset, are you?" I asked as I secured the yellow ribbon around her arm. "I'm sure we can trade with someone if you'd prefer to be on my team."

"Not at all." Her smile strengthened, and she helped me with my blue ribbon. "I'll have fun trying to find you."

And maybe I'd find her and steal a few kisses. The idea warmed me up nicely.

George beamed at the large group milling around him. "Questions?" After a short pause, he lifted his hand. "On three, the blue team will run. Yellow team? Get ready. Three . . . Two . . . And one!" His arm dropped.

After giving Luna a quick kiss, I shifted into my wolf form and raced into the woods with my friends, yipping with excitement.

CHAPTER 17

LUNA

"It's been ten minutes," George called out. "Yellow team? Go find those blues."

I ran down the wooded trail Storm had taken, but within a minute, I slowed to a walk. The sun had set and while the moon had risen, it was hard to see much of anything in the dense vegetation on either side of the trail. The wolves had the advantage with their higher sense of smell. But my hearing was good, and it wasn't long before the crackle of leaves to my right sent me in that direction.

I rushed up to Tayla, who I recognized in wolf form, wearing a blue ribbon still around her upper arm.

A tap on her shoulder, and she shifted into her human form, pouting.

"You found me so easily," she said with a huff she chased up with a smile. "Any sign of Escudek? He's on the yellow team."

"I heard him flying overhead at first but not lately."

She gazed around and sniffed the air. "I'll go look in the central meadow." A blink, and she was a wolf once more, bounding onto the trail and racing back to the central area.

Returning to the trail myself, I continued looking for Storm—or any of the blue team, for that matter. I tagged two more, one shifter and one man, and by then, I figured ten minutes had passed. It was time to return to the bonfire and get ready to hide so Storm could seek me.

I was moving along fast, chuckling about maybe letting him catch me so we could disappear during the hunt, when I rounded a bend in the trail and slammed into someone. Grabbing onto their arms to steady myself, I looked up.

Vincent.

My brother leered, his smile revealing his almost perfect teeth. The front left had a small chip in the left corner. I'd given him that when I was ten to his thirteen, when he trapped me inside a closet and wouldn't let me out. I'd remained there all night, huddled on the floor sobbing.

Eventually, he showed up to open the door. I flung a coat hanger at him, hitting him in the mouth. He started shoving me back into the closet, but I broke free and ran. I avoided him for the next month. If he caught up to me again, I wasn't sure what would've happened.

"Gotcha," he said, latching onto my upper arms. "Did you really think you could hide from me?"

I kicked out hard, hitting him in the shin. When he bellowed, reeling backward, I wrenched away from him. Bolting past him, I raced toward the clearing. If I was wise, I'd head in the opposite direction, leading him away from my friends, but fear turned me into a chipmunk to his cougar. All I could think of was finding Storm and begging him to hide me somewhere forever.

"Come back here," Vincent cried out, his footsteps stomping after mine. "You know I'll catch you. You'll never escape."

We'd see about that.

My heart roared up into my throat as I ran.

He gave chase, but all my running paid off, and I outdistanced him. If nothing else, I knew he wouldn't follow me into the open. He was the type who enjoyed gouging someone when no one else could see.

I burst from the forest and ran toward the fire, barely stopping before I plunged into its heated embrace.

Bent over, I braced my palms on my knees and struggled to catch my breath. My lungs wheezed, and my heart fluttered like a fly caught in a spider web.

Storm rushed over in wolf form, transforming as he reached me. He placed a warm hand on my spine. "Are you alright?"

Bitterness coated my tongue.

I'd dared to snatch a bit of happiness from the air and hold it close, but my brother would rip it from me and tear it to shreds.

I straightened and looked back toward the woods but

Vincent wasn't there. Yet he was. The weight of his gaze dragged me to the center of the Earth.

If I didn't run, he would grab me again.

This time, he'd make sure I never broke free.

CHAPTER 18
STORM

"I need to leave right now," Luna said, her grip on my arms tight enough to pinch. "Please. I have to get away." She shot a look of terror toward the forest.

"What's going on?" I asked. I stared toward the woods but saw nothing other than a few yellow team members striding out into the clearing, laughing about finding blue team members. A search with my wolf senses revealed others still inside the woods, shifters and humans. I couldn't narrow that down to individuals.

"Please." Tears streamed down her face. "Can you take me home? I need to . . ." A shudder ripped through her. "Please."

"Alright."

In no time, I drove my Jeep along the dirt road, taking us away from the pack meet-up, our hastily stuffed bags tossed in the back.

"Will you tell me what happened?" I asked. "I want to help you, Luna. I *need* to help you." The fear in her eyes when she peered toward the woods made me want to track down whatever frightened her and eliminate it forever.

"I can't. I'm sorry." Her voice came out clipped, but the look she shot me was full of sadness. She faced forward, her lips compressing into a sharp line. She held the tiny wolf carving on her lap, stroking it over and over.

I finally hit the main road and picked up speed, zipping along while watching my rearview mirror. No one appeared to be following, but I sensed whatever was bothering her back in town before we left had tracked her down at the pack meet-up. It had pinned her to the ground and made her fear for her life.

Her fingers remained locked on the sides of her seat, blanching from her tight grip.

Finally, I pulled up to her apartment and shut off the engine.

"I'm coming inside," I said. "We need to talk."

I was unbuckling when she gripped my arm. "Please. You can't. You have to leave."

Frustrated, I turned to face her, cupping her face. I was ready to go all alpha wolf and make her tell me what was going on so I could handle this, but the devastation in her eyes hit me in the guts like a sledgehammer. It knocked the wind from my lungs and smothered my irritation.

"Tell me," I said. "Please."

She leaned away from me and peered around, not turning back to me until she'd surveyed the entire area. I did the same thing but didn't see anyone watching or a reason for alarm. My wolf senses didn't pick up anything either.

"I don't have much time," she said, the words wrenched from her. "I thought we'd have a lifetime, but it's been stolen."

My heart shuddered, and I wanted to drag her onto my lap and hold her forever. I'd let no one and nothing near her. I'd protect her with the strength of my arms, the brutal grip of my wolf fangs, and the core of love burning for her within my heart.

"Come inside, but you can't stay long. I can't let him find you with me."

Him.

"Who are you afraid of?" I asked.

She placed a fingertip on my lips. "I'll tell you, just not here."

I grabbed her bag and followed her into her apartment. She took her bag from me and rushed to her bedroom, where she upended it, dumping out the contents. She rushed to her bureau and started pulling clothing out, stuffing everything into the case.

"Where are you going?" I asked.

"I have to leave. Don't you see?"

"I see you're scared. I want to help you, Luna, but I can't do that unless you tell me."

"I have to run!"

"Now?"

"As soon as I can." Her shoulders curled forward, and tears fell down her cheeks.

"Please let me help. Tell me what I can do."

"There's nothing anyone can do," she barked out.

I lifted my chin. "Then I'll go with you wherever you need to be. We'll run together."

"Storm." Her voice broke. "You can't come with me. I'm sorry."

"I see." I said the words by rote, but I didn't understand.

Moving past me, she peered out the window for a long while. "I'll explain, but I have to be quick."

She sunk onto her bed, and I sat with her, taking her hand. My thoughts raged, arriving at only one reason for her to push me away.

"You don't want me," I said.

"It's not that." She held my face, staring into my eyes. "I want you more than anything. It's just," her lungs hitched, "I can't be with you."

I tugged her onto my lap, warming her with my embrace. "Why?" I hated that I sounded desperate. Hurt. I shoved aside my feelings and focused on her.

"I . . ." She stared at my throat for a long time before looking up with so much sorrow in her gaze it made my heart shudder. "I come from a very wealthy family. A powerful family. You might even call them a bit like mafia in their own way."

"A dangerous family," I said, seeing where she was going with this. "And they're threatening you." A growl ripped from my throat, and if they were here, I'd lay waste until no one remained.

"My name isn't Luna," she said.

Shock plunged through me. "What's your real

name?"

She shrugged. "I'm Luna. *Your* Luna. She's the only person I want to be."

The moon chose her for me. I would trust in that above all else. "You're Luna, then." It was that simple.

"My family has controlled me all my life. They told me what to study at school, and they dictated how I spent my days. I could only be myself when I was with my mom." A sad smile filled her face. "We'd sneak away and just be us. Laugh, read what we wanted, and dream of a day when we were free."

"Where is she?" I asked, but inside, I already knew.

"She's dead. It was so sudden. She hadn't even been sick, and sometimes, I wonder . . ." Her eyes pinched closed before opening again. "I can't believe they'd go that far but look at what they're doing to me now. Chasing me. Stalking me. They won't let go!"

"I've got you," I said. "I'll keep you safe."

She shook her head. "Mom left me money, a big clump of cash tucked inside the cloth doll I always played with. Other than that, everything the family has belongs to the males, particularly my older brother, Vincent, who controls everyone and everything."

"You escaped."

She nodded. "So many times."

"And now you're living in Monsterville. You're a dog groomer. You run a pet boarding facility."

"I'm proud of myself. I've created the life I always wanted, the one me and Mom would've dreamed of. She loved animals as much as I did." A growl rose in her throat. "If only Vincent would leave me alone. But no, he had to control me like everything else. Before I ran this last time, he announced I would marry someone to form an alliance between our family and theirs." Her pleading gaze met mine. "Please understand. I want to help my family, but I couldn't do it. I'd heard about the guy. He's cruel and abusive. There are rumors . . ."

"Luna," I said, wrapping my arms tightly around her. I wanted to protect her from everything, but I was dealing with something beyond anything I'd heard of before.

"I took the money Mom secreted away for me and I ran." Her gaze fell from mine. "I'd barely started a new life when he caught me. He took me back and moved up the wedding date. The second time, I climbed out my bedroom window—he'd locked me inside. I clawed up over the roof and down a down spout, three stories to the ground."

"Luna," I sighed, knowing how scary that must've been. "I wish I could've been there to help you."

"Me too." Her sweet smile faded quickly. "That time, I traveled farther. As far as I know, I left no trail he could follow. But his henchman tracked me down. I escaped a third time and eventually made my way to Monsterville. This is the longest I've been free. But Vincent found me. He nearly caught me in the woods near the packs." She released a soft keen. "I love it here. I've found a home and my career makes me happy. Dogs are my thing, you know? When I'm with them, I almost feel complete." She stroked my face. "I'm only complete when I'm with you, Storm."

"Then stay. Don't run any longer."

"I can't. You don't know what Vincent's capable of. I'm not even sure I understand that fully. My father . . . I think Vincent killed him. I think he murdered our mother. And he'll kill me next if he can't force me into marrying that guy. If you try to come between us, he'll hurt you."

"Stay," I said again. "The moon has chosen. You're mine, and I'm yours."

"If only that could be true."

"It can be."

"I won't put you in danger. I can't risk you or the packs. Don't you see? He'll hurt them. He'll never give up until he has me in his clutches, and he won't come alone. He has his own equivalent of the packs, and there are many who are eager to do his bidding. With their help, he'll take me back. This time, he won't wait for a wedding. He'll call the priest and have the ceremony performed immediately. I'll be trapped forever."

Never. "It's not going to happen, Luna. I won't allow it."

"I wish there was a way."

"There is." Resolve filled me, and it wasn't long before I had the beginnings of a plan. "You know what we're going to do?"

She shook her head. "There isn't anything we can do."

"Sure there is," I said. "We're going to fight them."

CHAPTER 19

LUNA

I told him the truth, and he wasn't pulling away. But I was wrong to think I could steal happiness from fate, that I could have one brief bit of sunshine in my life.

"I'd love to stay and fight," I said. "I have so much to live for. You. Me. A world where we could love each other. It's too dangerous to try. I need to run before they find me." I tried to ease away from Storm, but he held tight, shaking his head.

"It's time to make a stand."

"He'll kill you!" My voice came out harsh and grating, but I'd shrivel up and die if my brother and his henchmen hurt him.

"I'm not killed that easily," he said. "You have a right to live your own life. No one can force you to do anything you don't want to do."

"He'll attack you. The packs if they're anywhere near me. That's why I had to leave." I flicked my hand in the direction of the mountains where the packs were probably still enjoying their wonderful weekend. "He'll plow through your friends like a dozer going through spindly trees, breaking and crushing every one of them."

"We're stronger than trees."

"That's not the point. He has a broad reach. He's powerful. He's cruel." My chest deflated. "Much too cruel. He needs that alliance, and he won't stop until he has me back in his clutches, ready to be handed over like a prize that belongs to him until he passes my rule to another."

Already, I'd taken too long to run. I should be at the bus station by now, buying a ticket with a fake name. I'd leave the bus before it reached its final destination and hitchhike or walk for a while, then take another bus and repeat the process over and over. I'd zigzag across the country until I was sure no one could follow.

"It doesn't have to be this way," he said. "Stay. We'll protect you."

I didn't have time to argue with him. My brother would wait for Storm to leave and pounce. If Storm remained much longer, Vincent would attack, and nothing would stop him from hauling me back to the city I came from.

"I know what you're thinking." Panic lifted my voice. "But what will protect you from him? He won't come alone. He'll bring many just like him. I've seen him do it. He lays waste until there's nothing left except smoldering ruins. He won't back down. Not ever. I'm the sacrifice he needs to further his own ambitions."

Storm eased me off his lap, but he held onto my

hand. I still clung to him like he was a lifeline. I should push him away, finish packing, and flee.

Instead, I wrapped my arms around him and struggled not to sob.

"It doesn't have to be this way," he said. "I promise you. There's a way through this, a way for you to be free to make your own choices in life." He tilted my chin up. "But in this, I am not going to dictate to you. I can't make you do what I want, because then I'd be just like your brother. Instead, I'm asking you to trust me. To place your future—*our* future—in my hands. We'll stand side by side and defeat him. He won't take you, and we'll make sure he can't make you do anything you don't want to do ever again."

I wanted to trust him. It would be so easy to place my life in Storm's hands instead of Vincent's. But he was right. This had to be my decision.

Storm was setting me free when my brother only brought chains, and that only made me love him more.

How long could I keep running? Each time, I depleted more of the money my mother left me. I worked when I could, but I hated abandoning each fresh start.

Maybe Storm was right. It was time to make my stand, to show my brother he no longer ruled me or my fate.

It was time to trust not just Storm, but the moon who had chosen me for him and him for me. We were destined for each other, and even Vincent could not sever the bond we'd formed.

I pinched my eyes shut as if I could shut out the world. As if I could close myself off and hide.

But that wasn't making a decision.

I opened my eyes and for the first time since my mom was alive, a sense of completeness filled me.

"I want to take a chance with you, Storm," I said. "I want to trust in us."

"Luna." He held me, the thud of his heart echoing within me. Easing back, he traced his fingers down my arms and linked our hands. "I'm going to call the packs. I'm calling my friends. You won't face them alone or with only me by your side." A feral gleam shone in his eyes. "We're *all* going to face them. We'll show them it's time they released you. We'll tell them you're going to live your life the way you choose."

CHAPTER 20

STORM

I placed a few quick calls, and everyone vowed to pass the word. They all said they'd help.

"We won't handle this here," I told Luna, taking her back out to my vehicle. A quick scan of the area didn't reveal anyone, but I sensed he was watching at a distance, waiting for her to act.

Vincent. Her enemy and mine.

"Where are we going?" Luna asked, gaping as I drove my Jeep from town as if the bats of hell were after us. Maybe they were. I'd heard a demon had moved to town. Perhaps he'd brought minions.

"I'll get you to safety and in the morning . . ." We'd finish this.

I gritted my teeth and kept my eyes on the road other than checking my mirrors to see if we were being followed. I sensed we were, though I hadn't seen any suspicious vehicles. Luna told me her brother and his henchmen drove black sedans with dark windows, so I studied every car or truck we passed.

Eventually, I darted my Jeep onto a logging road. I drove up over a rise and down, then shut the vehicle off.

"Be right back," I said, climbing out and hurrying to the gate installed near the road. Once it was locked, I crouched in the bushes as a wolf, watching and listening. A black sedan passed, followed by another. I waited ten minutes, and when they didn't return, I went back to my Jeep, starting it and slowly driving down the rutted road.

The passage turned into a slip of nothing, and I engaged the four-wheel drive, taking us deeper into the woods. Eventually, we came to the piece of land I'd inherited from my great-grandmother. I parked beneath a cluster of evergreens, got out, and used branches to disguise my vehicle. I doubted Vincent would find us here, but I'd keep an eye out all night long.

Luna stood beside the vehicle, her arms looped around her waist, shivering.

I tugged her into my arms and held her, murmuring soothing words that meant nothing and everything.

"We'll stay here tonight," I said softly.

"In the vehicle?"

"What are your thoughts about tents?"

She shot me a tremulous smile. "I like the idea of a tent if you're inside with me."

"Then let me show you." I took her hand and led her along a thin trail that ended at a wooden shed my great-grandfather had built a long time ago. Inside, I tugged out the two-person tent, setting it up beneath a broad evergreen branch. I inflated the mattress and pulled out the totes holding blankets, two small pillows, and sealed protein bars. A plastic gallon of water would see us through the night.

"I come out here about every three months," I said as I made our simple bed inside. "I replenish the supplies if the mice have found them and replace the water."

"Will we be safe here tonight?" The quake in her voice was like a minotaur hoof stomping on my heart.

"I'll make sure we are," I said. "Let's get you inside."

She clung to me. "You'll be with me."

"After I survey the area as a wolf."

Biting her lip, she nodded. She dropped to her hands and knees and crawled into the tent. "I'll be okay. Check things out and come back to me."

"Always, Luna. I promise."

In wolf form, I made careful, widening circles until I'd covered about ten miles around our tent, and I was grateful I found no evidence of Vincent and whoever he might bring with him. After waiting in the woods by the entrance for about twenty minutes and still not seeing or smelling anyone, I took the long way back to the tent.

When I climbed inside, she sat up and held out her arms.

I stripped quickly and joined her beneath the blankets, where I made tender love to her. After, I held her while she slept.

I wouldn't sleep. Remaining on guard was all that mattered.

At dawn, we packed up the campsite, washed down protein bars with water, and returned to my Jeep.

I took it back to town, driving slowly, and wound up and down multiple streets of Monsterville until I was confident we'd been seen.

With gritted teeth and a strong sense of vengeance scorching through my veins, I drove out of town.

"You're luring them," she said, peering backward. "He's remaining a few cars behind, but he's following. I see five vehicles. How in the world does he think we haven't seen him?"

"He's overconfident. I'm sure he believes there's nothing we can do."

"Is there?"

I took her hand. "Trust in us."

Her spine tightened, and she nodded. "I do trust in us. This is going to be okay. Where are we going?"

"Back to the central pack area," I said.

Her hands tightened on her seat. "We can't endanger your friends and family."

"We won't. They're getting ready. I promise, only those who wish to support us will be there."

She leaned back in her seat, though her posture remained tight. "My brother's about to get his eyes opened if he challenges a bunch of wolf shifters."

I flashed her my fangs. "We have a mean bite."

Her low laugh rang out, and I was grateful to see her posture loosen.

We arrived at the central pack area and parked well out of the way. I was pleased to note many vehicles had already arrived.

A glance back down the road revealed the dark sedans cresting a hill about half a mile away. They parked and got out, melting into the woods.

We didn't have long.

As we jogged up the trail, we met up with Gunner, Rylee, Max, and Chastity. Gunner, a huge orc blacksmith who'd recently moved to town with his wife, Rylee, carried an enormous hammer.

"Let 'em try to hurt your mate," he growled, hefting his hammer.

"This might sound silly," Rylee said from his side, hefting a bulging kitchen garbage bag. "But I brought cupcakes."

Luna's giddy laugh slipped out, but she cut it short with a hand over her mouth.

"I know, right?" Rylee said, chuckling. "Lately, I've been feeding my leftovers to the birds. I toss them into the freezer and bring them to the park on Sunday. They're like hockey pucks now, so your brother and his friends better watch out."

Luna gave Rylee a quick hug. "Thank you."

Rylee grinned. "I also brought some fresh ones to have for the celebration after it's all over."

"Her cupcakes are to die for," Chastity said. She patted the baby carrier strapped across her chest, reminding me she'd recently delivered her and Max's daughter, Sydnee.

"You, my mate," Max said gruffly, his arm protectively around his wife's back. His orc green skin gleamed in the morning sunshine, "are going to remain well behind the front line. Promise me this." In his other hand, he held a six-foot-long two-by-four.

Chastity shot me and Luna sad looks. "I want to fight alongside you, but I can't risk the baby. I'll be there to celebrate later, though."

And we *would* celebrate. I was confident this would end as it should.

"This is Raze," Max said, waving to an ogre wearing a business suit marching off to the side. "He runs a wedding planning business in town. My company built his new office building, and we're friends."

Raze gave me a curt nod and hefted a long, mini-sword letter opener and a three-hole punch. "Solid steel," he growled. I welcomed his brawn, but I wasn't sure about the office supplies turned weapons.

"Thank you," I said. "Perhaps you could protect Chastity?" That would get the businessman out of the way so he didn't get hurt.

His gaze narrowed, and flint filled his eyes. "Don't let the suit fool you. Battle roars through my veins."

Before they'd formed a treaty a hundred years ago, ogres had warred with orcs for generations. Were ogres still trained for battle? They must be. As big and brawny as Gunner, he may look uptown and sophisticated, but his spine must be as steely as his three-hole punch.

"And this is Vrok," Max said, waving to an orc

striding on the other side of Raze. Max gave quick introductions.

Vrok nodded. "Glad to be here to help." His grip tightened on a huge hammer. Like every other orc I'd met, he had dark green skin and black hair, but his eyes were golden, something I hadn't seen before.

"Thank you." I was grateful to my friends, and I owed them a huge meal at my restaurant when this was over.

"Don't forget me," a crotchety voice called out behind us.

"Grannie Vi," Rylee said, dismay lifting her voice. "You promised you'd stay back at the house." She glanced at me. "My grandmother is visiting Monsterville. She assured me she wouldn't get involved in this."

"What, you want me to miss out on all the fun?" Grannie Vi hobbled to catch up to us. She hefted her cane. "Let me at 'em. I'll teach 'em a trick or two."

"Stay with Chastity, please, Grannie," Gunner said softly. "They'll hide in the basement beneath the bathroom building. We wouldn't be able to bear it if something happened to her or the baby."

"A babe, you say?" Grannie Vi said, squinting Chastity's way. "Why in the world would you bring an infant to a battle?"

Why would a woman who looked at least eighty come to a battle herself?

"I'll make sure she stays safe," Rylee whispered to me, hurrying beside us.

"I heard that," Grannie Vi said. "And I won't have it. If Luna and Storm need help, I'm going to give it."

"Truly," Rylee said in a low voice. "I will."

"Grannie Vi," Chastity said. "Would you please stay with me? I don't believe I can protect my daughter alone."

"Well, of course I'm more than able to help on both fronts," Grannie Vi said. "Wouldn't want the bad guys to harm a hair on your beautiful daughter's head."

We left the path and walked out into the open clearing that looked stark and lonely without the bonfire and people dancing around it.

My heart expanded to see so many of my friends here to help us.

Gunner and Max took Chastity and Grannie Vi around to the back of the bathroom building to help them descend into the basement through the bulkhead and returned quickly.

Three gargoyles landed near George, who was organizing everyone along the edge of the meadow. We'd present a unified front.

Goreg held his wife, Violet. When he set her on the ground, the dogs she was dog sitting for Luna took off, breaking free.

Stella the Yorkie and Fred the Maltese raced across the clearing and leapt into Luna's outstretched arms.

Violet hurried over to us and grabbed their leashes. "Sorry. I thought I had them. They don't seem to enjoy flying much, which I can't understand." She shot Goreg a grin. "I fly with my husband every chance I can."

"Well, that was a treat," Violet's Uncle Bub said when Murtik, Goreg and Escudek's gargoyle brother, placed him carefully on the ground. Like Grannie Vi, Uncle Bub used a cane. "Can't say I've ever flown outside an air-o-plane."

"I'll take him to the others," Gunner said, sweeping Uncle Bub up in his arms and racing toward the bulk-head. He returned not long after, wiping his palms together, though he frowned as he stepped over to us.

"Problems?" Violet asked. "I could talk with Uncle Bub if he's not cooperating. He refused to stay home, promising he'd remain well away from the fight."

"He was quite fascinated by Grannie Vi," Gunner said, blinking slowly. "He said something about formally introducing himself and asking her out."

Violet snorted. "Leave it to my uncle to look for a date during an event like this."

"Weapons," George said grimly, going through the crowd handing out thick sticks, tools, and even an axe. "We wolves, of course, will battle with our claws and teeth."

Tayla strode over with her new mate, Escudek, who brandished a fence post.

"We are here to help you, Luna and Storm," he said, bowing formally in our direction.

Tayla hugged Luna. "You're a sister to me now. There's no place I'd rather be than with you at a time like this."

"Are we ready?" George bellowed. "I smell them coming."

They were about a quarter of a mile away, moving

carefully through the woods as if they thought wolves wouldn't hear them.

Fiona raced from the forest in wolf form, shifting just before she reached us. "I'm here," she panted. Her gaze swept from Luna to me. "You've been like a son to me from the time you were born, Storm. I'm going to help you defend your moon chosen mate."

"Fiona." Luna's eyes glistened with tears. "Thank you."

Fiona gave her a tight nod. "It's the least I can do after you helped my great-nephew."

More wolf shifters slunk from the trails, and it looked like half the packs were here. My heart swelled even bigger, and I squeezed Luna's hand as hope surged within my chest.

"You thought you'd face him alone, love," I said, tugging her into my arms. "But you have all of us by your side, not just now but always."

"I don't know what to say." Tears streaked down her cheeks, and I carefully wiped them away.

"Get your hands off my sister," someone snarled from within the woods. Vincent, of course. I'd smelled the taint of his corruption long before he spoke.

Luna's breath caught. "It's my brother." She lifted a shaky finger toward a muscular male striding from the woods with fifteen other males flanking him. They were all dressed in black. Sunlight glinted off their weapons, telling me they'd come prepared to fight.

No more threatening my mate.

With a snarl, I shifted and bared my teeth at Vincent.

CHAPTER 21

LUNA

"Hi-ya!" Grannie Vi cried, rushing from behind the bathroom building. As Vincent's men advanced, she swung out with her cane, smacking a henchman. The guy barely flinched, though he swore and stalked toward her.

She yelped and scurried back toward the building.

Uncle Bub hobbled forward from the shade and placed himself between them, the tip of his cane pressing against the henchman's throat. "Stand down you asswipe."

As far as threats went, it wasn't much, but Stella and Fred nipping at the henchman's ankles leant weight to Uncle Bub's words.

Vrok leapt between them, swinging his hammer through the air so quickly, it whistled. The guys paused, their eyes widening. Did they think we wouldn't defend ourselves and our friends?

"Leave the old people alone," Vincent said dryly, his

gaze focused solely on me, an unspoken threat coming through in his words. If I didn't go peacefully, he'd hurt my friends.

My brother's minions clustered behind Vincent. Grannie Vi snagged Uncle Bub's arm and they returned to the basement. I hoped they'd remain there, but Violet followed to make sure, tugging Fred and Stella with her.

Vincent surveyed those gathered with me, a mixture of snarling wolves and monsters. "I've come for Luna. I have no war with you folks." His dark gaze fell on me. "Come home with me, sister. Your fiancé is waiting."

I lifted my chin. In the past, I'd shriveled whenever he spoke to me. I ran and hid when he made threats.

It was over. I wouldn't let him rule me any longer.

"If you come peacefully, sister," he said. "There's no reason we need to . . . harm anyone."

One of his henchmen snickered. He lifted a pipe and brought it down onto his palm with a sickening smack.

The others held knives, baseball bats, and even a few broken bottles. My brother only brought guns when he intended to kill. He must believe I'd go with him, that this wouldn't turn into a real battle.

He was about to learn otherwise.

My resolve to stand up to my brother was weakening, however. I couldn't let him harm my friends.

Tears spilled from my eyes. I didn't want to go with him, but watching these wonderful people get hurt would crush me more than being forced to marry someone who might harm me.

"I'm sorry," I whispered to Storm as I took a step toward my brother.

A slick grin rose on Vincent's face. "Yes, that's right. Come to me, sister. We'll be on our way home before you know it."

A whoosh swept through the clearing, sending leaves scattering and making my hair whip around my face.

Murtik, Escudek, and Goreg flew down between us, landing with heavy thuds on the ground. They kept their wings extended, blocking us from my brother and his men.

Yelps rang out from my brother's henchmen. Perhaps they weren't so confident they could defeat wolves, orcs, ogres, *plus* gargoyles?

"We do not wish to fight," Escudek said. "But if you try to take Luna, we will end this, and you will not enjoy the results. Leave."

"Get them," my brother cried.

I couldn't see much around the gargoyles, but it was enough to chill my bones. My brother and his minions ran in this direction.

My wolf friends raced toward them with teeth bared and claws digging into the ground, with Storm in the lead. He passed the gargoyles who'd tucked their wings in and had engaged henchmen. Fists and claws smacked into the men dressed in black, and cries of pain echoed in the meadow.

Max and Gunner swung their weapons, barreling into men dressed in black.

Raze fought with concise precision, slicing with his

letter opener and spinning, hitting out with his heels and three-hole punch.

The gargoyles snatched up my brother's men and flew above the tree line before dropping them. Their cries of fear were followed by branches breaking and heavy thuds.

Frozen cupcakes flew through the air like softballs, impacting heads, and knocking a few henchmen down.

"Take that," Rylee cried, her voice echoing in the clearing as she lobbed a barrage of frozen cakes at the men.

I couldn't stand here while everyone else fought my battles. With my teeth clenched, I raced toward my brother, who grappled with Storm. Storm reared up, and his paws landed hard on Vincent's shoulders. His snout darted forward; his fangs bared to rip out Vincent's throat.

Crying in terror, Vincent clutched Storm's ruff, spinning and struggling to keep Storm from shredding his neck.

My mate had turned into a furious beast, determined to protect me even if it cost him his life.

I grabbed a stick off the ground. Scrambling around behind Vincent, I struck out, gouging the point into my brother's back.

He yelped and wrenched free from Storm, diving to the side and rolling to come up in a crouch.

Storm leapt on my brother, driving him to the ground again, snarling and tearing at the front of my brother's dark suit.

"Enough," a stony voice shouted.

I wasn't sure why everyone stopped fighting and gaped at the incredibly muscular, silver-skinned male who strode from the main trail and into our midst. Perhaps it was the unearthly glow shining behind his teal eyes. Or his thick, snake-like hair coiling and snapping around his shoulders.

When one of my brother's men stabbed out, trying to gut Max with a knife, the silver man turned his blue eyes the henchman's way.

"I told you to stop," the silver guy said. A gorgon? He must be. I hadn't seen him around town.

The henchman literally froze, his hand extended toward Max. His skin crackled and snapped as he turned to stone.

Within seconds, all but Vincent had been encased in pale gray stone, permanently fixed in whatever position they'd been in when the silver man turned his blue laser beam gaze their way.

"Darrow," Gunner said, dropping his hammer. "You're a welcome sight." He sneered at Vincent as he backed away to stand among his henchmen. He gaped at them. "What...? What...?"

Storm shifted back to his human form and came over to stand with me, wrapping his arms around me.

I lifted my jaw that had dropped when Darrow started shooting . . . I wasn't sure what had come from his eyes. Lasers? No, that couldn't be right.

"You're a gorgon," I whispered, and Darrow nodded. Anger and dismay lurked in his eyes, and I wondered about the dismay. He'd helped us, but would he pay the price?

My brother walked among his henchmen, stopping to touch one and then another. "They're . . . They can't be stone!" He spun to face Darrow. "What did you do to them?"

Darrow directed his gaze to the ground. "I stopped them. Would you like me to stop *you* as well?"

"Please don't. He belongs to me," Storm said, leaving me to advance on my brother. His hands shifted into claws. He'd shred Vincent to pieces, and I welcomed being free of my brother. I wouldn't mourn his death, but could Storm live with knowing he'd killed a member of my family even if my brother was complete shit?

I ran forward and grabbed Storm's arm, holding him back.

"Leave him," I said. I growled at my brother. "Go and don't return to Monsterville."

"You have to come back with me," my brother snapped. "I need you for the alliance."

I glared. "If you want someone to marry that horrible man, do it yourself."

My brother's gaze skimmed the ground, and a feral gleam appeared in his eyes. He snatched up a pipe and rushed toward Storm. "Come with me, or your lover dies."

"Well, this has been entertaining," someone said in a sardonic voice from our right. "But I believe I've seen enough." A male with burnished copper skin and thick horns arching up over his head strode from the woods beside us, his spiked tail twitching. He strode up to my brother, who had the sense to back away.

The pipe dropped from my brother's hands, and he lifted his arms, blubbering. "Don't . . . Who are you?"

"My friends call me Venom," the demon said with a slick smile. Something about him told me that he thrived on challenge, but that he rapidly defeated whoever took him on. "Since you're not a friend, you can call me Vengeance."

Venom looked my way, one of his dark eyebrows lifted. He splayed his hands and light gleamed on his claws. "Can I have Vincent, please?"

"I, um, sure." My thrill of excitement was smothered by horror. "What will you do to him?"

"I believe it's time Vincent got a taste of what awaits him at death," Venom said. He latched onto my brother's arm. A pop, and they disappeared, leaving nothing behind but the faint scent of smoke.

"Venom, huh?" My body shook, and my heart floundered in my chest. We'd come so close to being hurt or killed. All my oomph had fled from my veins, leaving only a shaky body behind.

When I staggered, Storm caught me and swept me up in his arms.

"Who was that?" I asked.

He grinned down at me. "Didn't I tell you a demon has moved to town?"

A demon? Whoa.

Around us, cheers erupted. Wolves shifted back to their human forms and danced around my brother's stone henchmen. The gargoyles took flight and soared above the meadow.

Darrow waved toward the stone men. "If you'd like, I'll be happy to take care of this mess."

"Will they remain stone forever?" I wasn't sure if I was horrified or happy about the idea.

"I've . . ." He pinched his gorgeous eyes shut. "I learned how to change the stony ones back, but I'll leave them in this shape for a while to give them time to think. Even in this form, they have complete awareness."

"That would be amazing," I said. The perfect solution. "Thank you."

Without Vincent giving directions, they'd return to the city. Some might turn in the opposite direction and run away wiser than when they came to Monsterville.

Vincent was the driving force behind the family. If he didn't return, someone would step into his place, but whoever took charge wouldn't bother to come after me, especially after the henchmen returned and shared what happened.

Who'd dare take on a monster army to capture one woman?

"Are you alright?" Storm asked, nuzzling my neck.

"Yup. You don't have to hold me."

"I want to. You once said life gave you too much and never enough. What are your thoughts now?"

"I have you. Our friends. Hell, a demon kicking my brother's ass." I kissed him and grinned, linking my arms around his shoulders. "I believe this time, I have more than enough."

CHAPTER 22

STORM
EPILOGUE

One Week Later

"Are you sure it's okay that we just stop by like this?" Luna asked in a hesitant voice as I parked my Jeep Wrangler in the driveway of Violet and Goreg's B&B. "They could be busy doing . . . something."

I shut off the engine, unbuckled both me and Luna, and levered my seat back as far as it would go. With a grin, I tugged her onto my lap.

"Love," I said. "How can you doubt how welcome you are not just in Monsterville but at Violet and Goreg's place?"

"I know," she said, wrapping her arms and legs around me as much as she could with the wheel at her back. "It's just . . . I'm not used to anyone sticking up for me. Even my mom could only do so much."

"You didn't run, which means you stuck up for yourself."

She nodded. "You're right. I know this. We did it together. My brother's henchmen came, and our friends helped me defeat every one of them."

I released a soft laugh. "We can mostly thank Darrow and Venom for that."

"You challenged Vincent." She leaned her head against my chest. "You were glorious. But Venom." Her voice went sly. "I think I've got a crush on our resident demon. All that bronzed skin. Those muscles." She peeked up at me through her lashes, mischief alive in her eyes.

I laughed. "You're getting nowhere with your teasing, love."

"You're right. He can't compare to you."

"Venom will keep your brother busy for some time, though I'm sure he'll be released eventually. And if Vincent dares to show his face here again, he won't just have our newly elected sheriff making sure he behaves, *I'll* handle him." I'd take Vincent deep within the woods and only one of us would walk out.

She frowned. "Who's the new sheriff?" Her eyes widened. "Oh, Venom?"

"No one ran against him." Who'd dare take on a demon? It was going to be interesting having a demon in charge of law enforcement. No one would step even an inch out of line.

"This is . . . amazing." The tension in her spine eased.

Violet and Goreg came out the front door and stood

on the top step. Catching my eye, Violet waved for us to come inside. I lifted my hand to show her I'd received her message.

"I still feel bad for bringing horror to our pretty town," she said, worrying her lower lip. "We were lucky no one was seriously hurt."

We'd sustained only a few cuts and bruises that they all brushed off. Everyone wanted to help Luna.

"Do you want to go have a picnic in the park instead?" I asked.

"There are three inches of snow on the ground." She'd made a snowman this morning and seeing her pink cheeks and glowing eyes when she showed her friend off made my heart come to a shuddering halt. I'd swept her up in my arms, kissed her until she moaned, and took her inside to warm her up.

My blood still sung from the magic we created together.

"If you want a picnic, I'll shift into my wolf form and snuggle beside you. That'll keep you warm."

She smiled at me. "Thank you."

"For what?"

"For making me smile. For making my life complete." She tilted her head, gazing up at me. "What are we doing sitting in a cold vehicle, Storm? We need to go inside!"

Laughing, we spilled out of my Jeep and strode up the walk.

"I was beginning to think we might have to come rouse you from your car," Violet said cheerfully. "You guys can make out later."

"Sure thing, Violet," I said, squeezing Luna's hand.

She squeezed back, telling me she would be up for making out later too.

We'd talked about moving in together. I had a cute little house where we spent most of our time, and she'd told me she'd picked up boxes from the supermarket and had started packing. Life couldn't get any better than this.

We climbed the front steps and entered the big, bright foyer behind Violet and Goreg.

"Welcome," Uncle Bub said, striding forward with the assistance of his cane. Grannie Vi held onto his arm, and when they got close, she gave me a wink and grinned at Bub.

You go, sweetheart. You go.

I gave them both a hug, as did Luna.

"Come on into the living room," Uncle Bub said, pointing his cane in that direction. "Why are you makin' them stand around in the foyer, Violet?"

She rolled her eyes and followed us into the big front room.

"Surprise!" a big group of people shouted.

"Oh, my." Luna cupped her face. Her eyes gleamed with tears as she took in our friends gathered to greet her, plus the banner, *Welcome to Monsterville, LUNA.*

"The paperwork isn't official yet," she whispered.

We'd gone to city hall last week to begin the process of legally changing her name to the one she'd chosen.

"You're Luna to us," Chastity said, striding forward with her newborn in a sling on her chest. The little girl was awake, and she cooed and kicked her feet. She looked just like her dad, from her green skin to her tiny tusks. Chastity gave Luna a hug around the baby and stepped back into Max's arms.

"I think it's wonderful that you chose Luna and now you're mated with a wolf shifter," Max said.

"In my heart," she said. "I must've known the name was perfect."

"You're perfect," I said, putting my arm around her shoulder and leading her around the room.

"I made cupcakes," Rylee announced. "Early this morning, that is. These aren't frozen ones like those we threw at . . ." She coughed. "Well, you know who."

"Thank you again," Luna said, tears streaming down her cheeks. Her grin showed the world how happy she was.

"Any time." Rylee smiled up at Gunner standing beside her. "We've started storing a few in the freezer just in case our new sheriff needs assistance."

I couldn't picture Venom eating a cupcake, let alone using a frozen one as a weapon, but maybe he had a soft side we'd yet to see.

Gunner shook my hand, and we thanked him too. Their toddler son rode on his left shoulder. The pup kept eyeing the cupcakes, and his face would soon be smeared with frosting.

"Raze sends his regards," Gunner said. "He had to leave to help plan a wedding in Petrified Woods."

"Help?" I asked. "Someone needed more than one wedding planner?"

Gunner shrugged. "The bride's friend was handling some parts and Raze the rest."

Two wedding planners, huh? Raze gave me the impression he could confidently handle anything. Someone like that might not enjoy sharing the job. Would fireworks shoot toward the sky? Maybe we'd hear about it later from Gunner.

George and Fiona hurried over to us and gave us hugs.

"I'm sorry for how I behaved when we first met," Fiona said, shooting me a contrite look. "I had no right to do what I did. You deserve happiness, Storm, and I'm glad you've found it with Luna."

"It's forgotten," I said, kissing her forehead. The bittersweet feeling I'd carried in my heart for Marlie was fading, replaced by sadness for her loss and hope for my new future.

"I can't thank you enough," Luna said.

We chatted with our friends, alternating eating from the buffet with standing in front of the fireplace, savoring the heat of the flames.

"I love it here in Monsterville," Luna whispered. She turned in my embrace and tugged my head down for a kiss.

"This is where you belong, love," I said, holding her precious face.

"You're right." Her teary gaze took in our friends laughing as we all hung out together. "I do belong here. In Monsterville, I've finally found a home."

I hope you've enjoyed Storm & Luna's story!
Check out the rest of the Monsterville, USA world...

Candy For My Orc Boss
(Max & Chastity)

Orc Me Baby One More Time
(Gunner & Rylee)
**If you've already read
Orc Me Baby One More Time
get your FREE BONUS Chapters!
Rylee & Gunner are having their baby!**

Gargoyles Just Want to Have Fun
(Violet & Goreg)
Uptown Ogre
(Raze & Elisa)

AND, if you'd like a peek at
Whose Bed Have Your Claws Been Under,
Darrow & Paige's story,
keep scrolling . . .

Want a FREE book?
Sign Up For My Newsletter!

& get Escorting the Alien,
a complete romance,
FREE!

About the Author

Ava Ross is a two-time *USA Today* Bestselling author who has written numerous titles, all of them featuring sweet and steamy romance. She fell for men with unusual features when she first watched Star Wars, where alien creatures have gone mainstream. She lives in New England with her husband (who is sadly not an alien, though he is still cute in his own way), her kids, and a few assorted pets.

SERIES BY AVA

Mail-Order Brides of Crakair

Brides of Driegon

Fated Mates of the Ferlaern Warriors

Fated Mates of the Xilan Warriors

Holiday with a Cu'zod Warrior

Galaxy Games

Alien Warrior Abandoned

Beastly Alien Boss

Bride of the Fae

AVA ROSS

A Sci-Fi Holiday Tail

Monsterville, USA

Monster on Board
(co-written with Alana Khan)

A Monster Worth Fighting For
(Monster Between the Sheets)

Third Galaxy on the Left

You can find my books on Amazon.

WHOSE BED HAVE YOUR CLAWS BEEN UNDER

**My ex-boyfriend was transformed into
a medusa, and he's set his eyes on me.**

Ten years ago, I was convinced I'd one day marry my high school boyfriend, Darrow. But when a mad scientist experimented on him and others in Petrified Woods, they were changed into monsters. My parents dragged me from town before I could make sure Darrow was okay. Not long after that, they told me he 'ddied.

Now I'm back in Petrified Woods to be the maid of honor at a friend's wedding. And guess who's the best man?

Darrow.

He's not dead.

He's mad at me for leaving him.

And his steely gaze could slice through my heart with a single glance.

Whose Bed Have Your Claws Been Under? is a part of the Monsterville, USA Series. Each book is standalone but is best if read in order. Expect romantic hijinks with monsters, heat, and a happily ever after.

Check out the entire Monsterville world!

Candy for my Orc Boss
Orc Me Baby One More Time
Gargoyles Just Want to Have Fun
Don't Go Knotting My Heart
Whose Bed Have Your Claws Been Under?
Uptown Ogre
Oops, I Elf'd it Again
My Orc-y Breaky Heart
Hold Me Closer, Fiery Phoenix
Who Let the Demon Out?

Get your copy NOW!

CHAPTER ONE
PAIGE

"Aw, you look gorgeous," I told my friend, Monica. She stood in front of a long mirror in one of the twenty-five bedrooms in the castle venue, her slim body encased in a white wedding gown fit for a princess.

Poppy, her orc-green face tight with excitement and tension, fluffed Monica's dress and made a few last-minute alterations, though really, the dress was perfect already.

"You think so?" Monica said, her teary gaze traveling from mine to Poppy's in the mirror. "I keep seeing pictures of my mom wearing this dress when she married my dad, and now I'll wear it when I walk down the aisle and into Trevor's arms. Thank you so much for helping with the alterations, Poppy." She hugged our friend, and Poppy beamed, her cheeks darkening. "If only Mom could be here to help me get ready. If only Dad was here to walk me down the aisle, though I'm honored Gunner agreed to do so."

Gunner was Poppy's older brother and a good friend of the groom.

With Monica's mom dead, she only had me, her best friend from high school and Poppy to be with her during this wonderful moment in her life.

I carefully blotted away her tears. "None of that, now. I know crying's a common thing at weddings, but don't ruin your make-up until after you've joined Trevor at the altar."

Nodding, she bit down on her trembling lower lip and smoothed the front of her gown. It had been made of the finest silk and tulle and had intricate beading and lace along the bodice. The skirt flowed out behind her, and Poppy had promised to hold it up so it wouldn't drag on the way to the chapel.

I stepped back. "You look wonderful. Trevor's going to be the one crying when he sees you walking down the aisle."

Elisa, Monica's wedding planner, murmured agreement from where she stood nearby.

"Thank you so much for being here with me, Paige," Monica said. "I know we only reconnected six months ago, but it means everything to me."

"There's no place I'd rather be. Now let's get to that church so you can get married," I said with a big smile.

The door opened behind us and the owner of the castle venue, Bart, a minotaur, poked his head in. "It's time." His gaze swept across us and remained on Poppy. Color climbed into his fuzzy cheeks, and his hooves drummed on the floor.

Poppy hid her grin. Those two. I shook my head. They'd been making eyes at each other since we arrived this morning. Romance appeared to be in the air for more than one couple.

Not for me. I'd had my chance ten years ago when I was sweet sixteen and he died.

Monica latched onto my arms and hopped in place. "I'm about to become Trevor's bride!"

I was surprised when she asked to be her maid of honor, though touched. When my family fled Petrified Woods, I never looked back. The memory of that time still haunted me.

A mad scientist kidnapping Darrow and other townspeople to experiment on them. They escaped, but they were never the same again . . .

Darrow texted me after he escaped, telling me he didn't feel right. Something was terribly wrong. He was scared.

My parents wouldn't let me go see him, stating I had to let the medical people deal with it.

It wasn't long after that we heard screams echoing through our small town, and whispers of *monsters*.

My terrified parents packed up all our possessions and fled the next night. This was the first time I'd returned to Petrified Woods.

"You're gorgeous, sweetheart." Poppy fluffed Monica's veil. At her nod, Monica smiled and started toward the door.

"I'm so glad I found you on Facebook," Monica said.

As Bart opened the door all the way, I handed Monica her glorious bouquet.

"If you hadn't found me, I never would've returned to town." How could I when Darrow died? When my parents told me, I collapsed. We'd been best friends since we were little. We'd even teased each other about getting married one day. We'd only kissed, but I knew who I wanted to be with for my first time.

My dreams died along with him.

We left the room and followed Elisa down the grand staircase. Bart waited at the bottom, red capes hanging over his arm.

When we reached him, he draped one around each of our shoulders. With Poppy, he paused and loosely tied a white bow beneath her chin. He stood there, staring at her while she did the same, and I began to think we'd be gray before we arrived at the church.

"Guys," Monica said with a laugh. "Later, okay?"

Poppy blushed. Bart stumbled backward, nearly tripping when one of his hooves caught on the rug.

"I apologize," he said, giving us a bow. His hooved hand swept out. "Please."

The chapel was located behind the castle, though the reception would be held in the grand ballroom spanning half the second floor. We crossed the foyer, continued down a hall and paused at the rear entrance door.

Bart clumped around us and opened it.

Stepping outside, I paused on the big stone deck to suck in a breath of crisp, wintery air. Poppy juggled Monica's train, making sure it didn't fall in the snow.

Monica grinned my way, her tears gone. "I can't wait to marry Trevor."

And from what I'd seen last night at the rehearsal dinner, he felt the same.

The only person missing from the dinner had been the best man. I wouldn't meet him until the wedding, though it didn't matter. Once the wedding weekend was over and Monica and Trevor left for their honeymoon in two days, I'd drive away from Petrified Woods and never return again.

"He's a medusa," Monica had whispered, though not in shock. After all, she was marrying an ogre. "He has snake-like hair that has a life of its own, though it's kind of sexy. It's silver," she'd said. "As is his skin, though that's a lighter color. He's kind of cute if sad." She'd frowned. "I think something horrible happened after he was changed, but no one's said a word about it to me. He's a sculptor and rather ironically, he runs a statuary." She'd released a high-pitch giggle. "Get it? Gorgon. Statuary? I asked Trevor once if he poured his statues or . . . created them."

"Created them?" I'd asked.

"You know," she'd said in a hushed voice. "Used his laser eyes to turn them to stone."

I wasn't sure what to believe, but I'd meet him soon. I didn't know any sculptors, let alone guys who could solidify others with a glance from their eyes.

Leaving the deck, we walked along a garden path with Bart leading.

"Everything's so beautiful," Monica exclaimed,

stroking the red bows decorating an evergreen tree. The place looked like a holiday wonderland, and I was happy for my friend. I couldn't imagine a prettier place to get married.

Sunlight filtered through the tall, spiky trees, making the light dusting of snow we'd gotten last night sparkle. The sweet essence of pine mixed in with the scent of cinnamon and cloves. Birds chirped as we passed, and I expected one to swoop down and land on Monica's finger, completing the forest princess image she projected.

We walked across a small stone bridge spanning a babbling brook, pausing to watch the water trickle over rocks and gurgle where ice was starting to form.

"It's lovely here," I said.

"Thank you," Bart said, clop-clop-clopping beside me on the path. "I inherited the estate from family, and decided it was the perfect place for a wedding venue." His gaze slid to Poppy, and she sidled closer to him.

"When Trevor asked me to marry him," Monica said. "I knew we had to get married here. I've ridden my bike past this place for years, dreaming of walking through the grounds and sleeping in one of the beds."

Bart gave her another bow. "We're delighted to help make your day special."

I couldn't imagine what it cost, but Trevor's family owned the country club, and Monica was a graphic designer in high demand. They could probably afford it.

Not me, but I didn't plan to get married. My heart was ripped from my chest ten years ago, and I hadn't found anyone who could step into the gap left by Darrow's death. It might be silly to mourn someone I hadn't seen for so long, but that was me, steadfast and loyal, as my mom always said. It made me a great lawyer.

We approached the big, stone church, and I marveled at the stained-glass windows on either side of the two-story doors. Organ music drifted through the air. Monica wanted a traditional wedding, and the formal march would soon herald her arrival.

"Oh," Monica called out, her eyes sparkling with tears again. "It's almost time." She smiled and hugged me, then Poppy, who still juggled Monica's train.

Two staff members dressed in black suits bowed to Monica, then swept open the double doors for her to enter.

She strode inside, her head held high and her spine stiff with pride while I scooted behind her, trying to look dignified while holding a basket full of rose petals. Without a flower girl, the job of sprinkling them on the aisle had fallen to me.

Inside the foyer, Elisa took our capes and fluffed our dresses.

We waited while the ushers approached the interior door.

Bart plodded to the right and opened a small panel, giving the signal that the bride had arrived and the wedding could begin.

Organ music grew louder, the melody a joyous fanfare that made my heart soar along with it. Long ago, I'd planned to walk down the aisle like Monica, only

Darrow would be waiting at the altar with a big grin on his handsome face.

Bart turned to Monica. "Ready?"

She nodded solemnly. "I am."

Poppy ensured her train was perfectly smooth, then stepped around her to enter through a side door with Bart and Elisa following.

The ushers opened the door to the chapel. The music rose, almost too loud.

Easing around Monica, I stepped onto the red carpet runner stretching between the pews, and started tossing petals, taking care not to throw too many. The basket was small, and I was supposed to hold back enough to throw onto the alter where Monica would stand with Trevor.

Peeking up, I took in Trevor gazing with complete adoration at Monica. Tears glistened in his eyes, and my heart squished for my friend. They'd be so happy together.

His best man stood to his right, though he hadn't turned to look. The silver, snake-like hair Monica had described was pulled back in a thick bunch at his nape, the long strands dangling past his shoulders. Did a person cut living hair or let it grow as long as it liked? Tall, he towered over Trevor who was six-three. His shoulders were equally broad, tapering to a narrow waist. He had a nice butt, something I shouldn't be noticing.

Monica sniffed.

I paid attention to where I threw the rose petals.

When I reached the altar, I stepped to the side and tossed petals on the smooth surface. I waited for Monica to join Trevor in front of the Reverend, then fluffed her train and made sure her gown lay smoothly. Taking her flowers, I stepped up beside her.

I glance toward the best man, wondering what he looked like from the front. Was he as gorgeous face-to as he was from behind?

Shock poured through me, and I released a guttural groan.

Monica glanced my way, but I couldn't drag my eyes away from him.

Darrow.

Pick up Whose Bed Have Your Claws Been Under NOW!

www.ingramcontent.com/pod-product-compliance
Lightning Source LLC
Chambersburg PA
CBHW021532150726
47990CB00006B/2209